CANDLELIGHT VICTORIAN SPECIAL

CANDLELIGHT REGENCIES

The Heart
of the
Matter

Diana Burke

A CANDLELIGHT VICTORIAN SPECIAL

Published by
Dell Publishing Co., Inc.
1 Dag Hammarskjold Plaza
New York, New York 10017

Dell ® TM 681510, Dell Publishing Co., Inc.

ISBN: 0-440-14208-3

Printed in the United States of America

First printing—December 1980

The Heart
of the
Matter

CHAPTER ONE

"Now see here, Miss Cressley, you needn't condescend to me! I try to give you the benefit of thirty years' experience, and you say you'll consider my idea carefully. Cheek! That's what it is!"

Miss Cressley's brown eyes gave away nothing and her lips remained curved in a pleasant smile. "Colonel Pucey, what more can I say? I do appreciate your concern, but you must realize that I have investigated the matter thoroughly as well."

"So. You'll go your own way as usual. Your father must be turning in his grave at this latest nonsense of yours. Do you want to ruin the company, girl?"

The colonel was shaking with indignation, his moustache bristling alarmingly. Miss Cressley might have feared he was about to expire of apoplexy if she had not seen him in like case so often before. Now her expression merely hardened at his daring to invoke her father's ghost.

"The business is doing quite well, Colonel, according to the latest quarterly report. Even you were pleased with your dividends. As for my father, we can't know how he feels about the way I run his company. My guess is that he might be rather proud of me. But I mustn't keep you any longer; you must have a great deal to do this morning."

The doors of the managing director's office swung violently outward, and a small man with a red face and a shock of gray hair came rushing out. Pulling himself up short beside the desk of the executive secretary, he glared at her truculently as he donned his gloves. "She's impossible!" he growled. "Quite impossible! There's no reasoning with her at all!"

Miss Hodgekiss watched his hasty departure with unmoved detachment, as the colonel was often in a rage. An important stockholder, he had never resigned himself to the fact that the board had chosen a woman over himself to head the affairs of Cressley Limited.

In the modern, industrial Manchester of 1895, Regina Cressley was a unique figure. Women were unknown in the world of finance. Although a few lucky ones might be the recipients of dividends, they did not create them. Regina was the exception.

When her father died twelve years before, leaving the bulk of his shares in the company he had founded to his only child, he fully expected her to sit back and reap the benefits of his endeavors. With judicious calculation Walter Cressley had not left her controlling interest, but rather enough to insure her lifelong comfort. He never dreamed that the chit would presume to step into his shoes and try to run the company herself.

It had taken years and great perseverance on

her part, but eventually the board members learned that Regina's ideas had an uncanny knack for making money, and they finally rewarded this valuable talent by electing her managing director of her own company. In a cautious way the directors cherished a certain pride in their unusual leader. They did find it strange that a woman should claim to know how to read a balance sheet, but the fact that the business grew from a small manufactory to a sizable holding company was proof enough that she knew what she was about.

There was one holdout on the board: Colonel Fitzgerald Pucey, a blustery little man, much given to snorting and chewing on the ends of his moustache. He had been a constant thorn in Regina's side ever since the board asked him to resign as pro tem manager so that they might replace him with another Cressley. That his many attempts to unseat her were unsuccessful was due largely to the allegiance of John Lassiter, a close friend of Walter Cressley's and a staunch supporter of his daughter. John was not much involved in the business and recognized early on that it was best left to Regina. Lately he had been talking of selling his shares, and Regina had quickly offered to buy, as the acquisition of John's stock would make her majority stockholder at long last. Lassiter had received a second nibble almost immediately from a London company, Jeremy Thwait and Associates of Barnstaple Street. Since Pucey had had some business dealings with Thwait in the past, it seemed he had alerted them that the stock might soon be available, evidently hoping that with their support he might regain control of the company. But Regina had great faith in Lassiter's integrity; he'd never sell his shares to someone else under those circumstances.

When Miss Hodgekiss brought in the mail and laid it with a discreet cough on her employer's desk, Regina did not look up.

"Thank you, Dottie."

Miss Hodgekiss gazed at the woman behind the desk with an affection not unmixed with awe. Dressed severely in a blue serge skirt, a white shirtwaist with leg-o'-mutton sleeves, her dark brown hair drawn tightly back into an unbecoming topknot, Regina Cressley clearly did not make any concessions to her femininity. At thirty-two she judged herself far too involved in more important matters, as well as being long past any need to gild the lily. Indeed, she would have been dismayed to learn that even her sensible garments could not wholly disguise her elegant figure, nor a habitually businesslike efficiency hide the warmth in her light brown eyes. Still, for the most part, her authoritarian manner deceived the world almost as much as it fooled Regina herself.

"There is a letter here you should look at immediately, Miss Cressley."

"File it with the others."

"How do you know what it is? I haven't said a word about it yet," asked her secretary.

"I can smell Aunt Pen's distinctive scent."

Drawing herself up to her full five feet, Miss Hodgekiss folded her arms across her ample chest. "Miss Wingarten is bound to be hurt by your disregard."

"Then send her a check."

"Miss Cressley!"

Familiar with that tone, Regina resigned herself to battle. Dorothy Hodgekiss was attempting to quell her in the same manner she had once used to subdue unseemly behavior in the schoolroom. It was, after all, Penelope Wingarten who had found Miss Hodgekiss starving genteely between jobs and arranged this position for her with Regina. Delighted to escape from the confining and ill-paid life of a governess, Miss Hodgekiss had accepted the challenge and turned herself into a model of office efficiency, more than justifying Miss Wingarten's faith in her. It was only at rare intervals that her tutorial tendencies came to the fore, but sometimes her employer invited the same stern rebuke as did a fractious child.

Regina forestalled her. "Dottie, I am terribly busy. Leave it and I'll read it later. Besides, I know what it says."

"A letter from one's great-aunt should rate some priority." *Especially if that great-aunt is Penelope Wingarten,* Miss Hodgekiss added silently. She felt a deep loyalty to the woman who had so radically changed her life. And indeed, Miss Wingarten was worthy of respect. One of the initial members of the Women's Suffrage Committee formed in Manchester in 1865, now, at age eighty, she was still a formidable advocate of women's rights.

Regina's secretary and great-aunt were united in urging the younger woman to take an active role in campaigning for the Cause. But Regina excused herself from participating, claiming she had no time for politics.

Her secretary's reproachful look stirred Regina's conscience. "Money can talk better than I can, Dottie. I'll pay for the rental of Albert Hall and travel expenses for one of your best speakers. Just think what can be accomplished in London."

"You cannot buy a clear conscience, Miss Cressley. Why, if it weren't for your great-aunt and others like her, you'd be . . ."

"I know, I know. Stuck away in some man's bedroom, awaiting his pleasure."

That shocking statement sent Miss Hodgekiss into a rosy confusion.

"I never . . . why, that's completely . . . Miss Cressley!"

Regina was amused, as always, by her emancipated secretary's outdated notions of propriety. "Would you have me wear bloomers for the Cause?"

The vision of her very proper employer appearing before the company directors in such garb was enough to raise the stain on Miss Hodgekiss's face to bright crimson. Her mouth opened, then snapped shut again. Miss Cressley sometimes said such outrageous things that it was difficult to keep one's composure. Sniffing eloquently, she retired to the outer office, her back stiff with disapproval.

Regina smiled to herself and tried to get back to the pile of work on her desk, but the reproachful letter stared at her with unwinking resolution, making it impossible to concentrate on the latest quarterly figures. Taking the ivory letter opener, Regina slit the seal. It would take only a moment to read after all.

Rowan House
Billingham
Dorset

Dear Regina:

I have just received the most shocking news from your cousin Celia. She is to be betrothed. I am so distressed; the child is barely out of the schoolroom!

What that fool of a father can be thinking of I have no idea, but I have placed no value on his understanding since the day he informed me he was to take holy orders.

Celia did not complain of her fate directly, but the child clearly has serious reservations. It seems her young man has fallen in with bad company, and his father believes that the influence of a good woman will save him. I'm sure that you agree that Celia deserves better than that.

I would go down to Surrey and put a stop to it myself, but I am leaving the country tomorrow. The literary women of Brussels have engaged me to speak at their convention. My topic is "Women's Challenge to Male Dominance in the Publishing Field."

Since I cannot go to Grantly, you must. It is imperative that we prevent your cousin from making a tragic mistake. Despite the fact that you have not answered my last three letters, I remain,

Affectionately yours,
Penelope Wingarten

Regina was at first amused at this typical example of Pen's florid chirography, but then, despite its exaggerated tone, the letter struck a responsive chord.

No one had dared try pushing Regina into marriage, but she well remembered feeling that it was expected of her. Many a suitor had come calling on the wealthy Miss Cressley, but she had rejected them, one and all, to her mother's lasting disappointment. Regina had preferred spinsterhood—and independence.

She never regretted her decision, though once she was tempted to discard her principles for a quickening of the pulses. But that weakness was soon overcome, and she never allowed any man that close to her again. In recent years the queue had disappeared anyway. It had become clear that Regina was married to her business, and even the most determined fortune hunter gave up

14

in despair. Besides, a middle-aged spinster whose heart was as cold as a quarterly profit margin was not the sort to tempt an ordinary man.

Regina thought of her own lucky escape from the constricting bonds of matrimony and realized again that Pen's example and moral support had been necessary ingredients in her decision. Now her great-aunt was asking Regina to do the same thing for some other unfortunate girl.

Although they did correspond, irregularly to be sure, Regina had not seen Celia since she and her father had left Manchester to live in a little village in Surrey five years before. That would make Celia barely seventeen. A child still, as Pen said, and much too young to make such a commitment.

A sense of outrage at what pressures Celia must be undergoing made the formidable Miss Cressley bristle with indignation. Uncle Arthur was an ass, though Celia didn't seem to have much more backbone herself. Still, she had appealed to Aunt Pen, and that did say something for her intelligence. No Cressley could be coerced without some sort of fight, and Celia, it seemed, was a Cressley underneath her docile acceptance of what must be totally repugnant to her. The girl was incredibly young to be forced into such a situation. Even the strong-willed Regina at that age might not have escaped without the help and guidance of her emancipated aunt.

Love was for the unenlightened, like Regina's own sweet, tractable mother, who couldn't understand any other way of life. But for a woman of

15

strength it was an intolerable situation. To be beholden to a man for every penny, for every consideration, was to give up one's very soul.

Regina put away the papers on her desk. They could wait; Celia could not. It was the least she could do for Aunt Pen and her unhappy little cousin. Regina herself would go to Grantly.

The committee meeting was over, and as usual, the problem had been tabled once again. Alistair Llewellyn Debenham, fifth Earl of Grantham, gathered up his papers and headed for his office. He was disappointed but not surprised at the committee's refusal to support his bill to introduce women's suffrage.

Many had hoped for the inclusion of women's enfranchisement in the Reform Bill of 1884, but Gladstone's immovable opposition had been too much to overcome then. Now the mention of women's rights brought only yawns and derisive laughter on the floor. Poor Margaret would be cast down at the news, the earl thought philosophically. He had frequently tried to explain to his sister the intricacies of Parliamentary politics—the dealing, the trading of votes, the struggle with entrenched procedure—but Margaret was impatient with all that.

"What can they fear when it is only justice we ask? Why should women be classed with the criminal and insane?" Rhetorical questions were rather Margaret's forte. "I can't understand why it is taking so long. We have many friends in Parliament. Are you trying really hard, Alistair?"

Margaret Debenham tended to overrate her brother's influence. Although he was liked and respected in the House of Lords, the more conservative of the peers discounted his opinions on many issues. "Bit of a crank," they said tolerantly or intolerantly, depending on their political complexion. "One of those sympathetic types, too soft-hearted to see what pernicious nonsense all this coddling of the lower classes is."

Lord Grantham smiled, albeit grimly. Yet things were changing for the better, even if it was with agonizing slowness. Last year's reform bill had been an excellent piece of legislation, and he could take pride in some of its provisions. The introduction of national safety standards in the mines, although a long way from ideal, was a step in the right direction. As for women, they would get the vote eventually, he believed.

Chuff met him at the door. "How did it go, my lord?" he asked respectfully.

"It didn't," grunted the earl, handing his office manager a sheaf of papers. "Better file these, Chuff. We shan't be needing them for a while."

"Very good, m'lord. Are there any further instructions?"

"No. Just shut up everything and be off, all of you. You'll be in Torquay with your daughter, I take it? Yes, well, have a good summer. I won't need you back here until the first of September.

17

Give my regards to Mrs. Chuff and your daughter, if you please."

"Thank you, m'lord."

Chuff watched as his employer said good-bye personally to the office staff. The earl was a fine-looking man and a pleasure to work for, as he was never too busy to exchange a friendly word. It was a shame he had never married; not that the ladies didn't dangle after him, but he seemed disinclined to change his life-style. He enjoyed certain temporary liaisons, but they didn't make up for the lack of a wife to come home to each night. The earl must have been thwarted in love as a young man, Chuff reasoned romantically. Yet the years have a way of creeping up on you. Why, his lordship's hair was white at the temples these days; he must be almost forty, was Chuff's startled thought.

If Chuff was protective of Lord Grantham and a bit concerned for him, it was only because he thought the earl too involved with his work and not attentive enough to his own personal needs. His lordship would miss dinner just to listen to a bunch of raving radicals. For instance, Chuff hadn't delayed Lord Grantham's departure by telling him about the delegation that had come calling earlier this afternoon. A group of funny ones, was Chuff's private opinion, and they could just wait until summer was over and the office open once again. "The Society to Prevent Motor Cars from Entering Villages of Less Than Three Hundred Souls and Disturbing Their Peace and

Tranquility." How the earl would laugh at that! Why, his own place was outside just such a little community. That's where he was off to now— Grantly.

The Daimler engine coughed twice, spat out a black cloud from its exhaust, and died with a convulsive jerk. The passenger, well-muffled in a long duster and protective goggles, shuddered in distaste and, with heroic self-control, forbore to complain.

Young Tom pulled off his hat and wiped a red and streaming brow before attempting to turn the crank once again. "She'll start in a flash, Tristam, once I get the motor turned over. There's a trick to it I haven't quite mastered yet."

"Don't mind me, Dawlish. I'm sure this will all make an amusing anecdote one day," came the rather daunting answer.

One more enormous heave and the motor roared into life, causing the chassis of the car to joggle vigorously. Beaming, Tom leaped into the driver's seat, opened the throttle, and released the brake. The automobile progressed down the road forthwith in a series of small convulsions, causing consternation to horses, cabmen, and passersby, who moved hurriedly out of the way.

Tom Dawlish was thrilled. "Ain't she a beauty!" he yelled happily into his companion's ear. "She'll do fifteen miles per hour on a straightaway."

"Undoubtedly, dear boy. Remind me to take the train next time, won't you?"

Tom was amazed and a little hurt. "You don't like it?" he shouted incredulously.

"It will be a unique experience, I feel sure." The irony of that remark passed over Tom's head, and he smiled contentedly at his passenger.

Barclay complained, "It is a bit like traveling in a boiler factory."

"What? I can't hear you," Tom answered at the top of his lungs.

Barclay shrugged a pair of well-padded shoulders. No *bon mot* could be witty when screamed over the devilish noise of this contraption.

The next hour was spent in silence. No, that was hideously untrue. Rather, the conversation languished. Even when the engine inexplicably died, and Tom spent a blissful half hour tinkering with it before it just as inexplicably revived, Barclay simply reclined in the shade of an ancient oak, his hat over his face. His only reply to Tom's breathless apologies was to say that a motor car's most appealing feature was its tendency to break down.

"Wake up, Tristam. She's ready to go!"

"So soon," Barclay said regretfully and climbed with stoic calm back into his seat.

Tom was perplexed. What could be eating Tristam? The poor fellow was out of sorts and with the best will in the world, Tom couldn't see why.

Bumping and backfiring down country lanes, frightening horses, being chased by barking dogs and boys who shouted, "Get a horse!" seemed to

Tom Dawlish the most delightful adventure of his life. Of course, Tristam was made of finer stuff and was altogether more sensitive than most people. In fact, Tom wasn't quite sure why Tristam Barclay, man about town and published poet, wanted to be his friend, but Tom was grateful anyway. Ever since Tristam had bought Honeysuckle Cottage and made their small village his second home, filling the converted rooms with all sorts of gay entertainment, Tom had become his humble devotee. Maybe Tristam wasn't out of sorts, just thinking up a new poem. As this explanation for his friend's silence occurred to him, Tom brightened up considerably. Besides, he was too happy at the thought of going home with his new motor car to worry about anything for long. Celia would be so excited, she was bound to forgive him for running off to London without saying good-bye. His father's reaction to Tom's new acquisition was another matter. Never mind. Tom couldn't wait to see everyone's face when he drove this beauty down the main street of Grantly.

CHAPTER TWO

An eddy of smoke and the smell of burning met Celia as she entered the vicarage kitchen. Dropping her armload of yellow roses on the table, she quickly removed a tin from the smoking oven; the scones were well-charred and quite inedible. With an exclamation of annoyance, she dumped the burnt offerings into the trash and propped open the door to the garden. Cousin Regina would have to settle for cucumber sandwiches for tea. The Cressleys' housekeeper was notoriously distractable, and the sudden news that company was coming to stay had disordered her wits entirely.

Regina's wire had arrived only hours before, throwing Mrs. Gatchell into an even greater state of disorganization than usual. Yet despite her faults, she was a good-hearted woman and had been with the Cressleys since Celia was a baby. The vicar thought her indispensable, though Celia sometimes wondered if it would not be easier to manage without her bumbling efforts.

Cheerful in spite of burned scones and smoke-reddened eyes, Celia arranged the roses in a silver pitcher. It was exciting and marvelous that Reina was coming to Grantly at last. If she had only given a little more notice. . . . As it was, Celia was doubtful about the adequacy of the dinner that night. Though she had sent Mrs. Gatchell out for more chops, it was not exactly going to be elegant. Most days the fare at the vicarage ranged from frugal to plain and healthy. Mrs. Gatchell's talents did not run so far as gourmet cooking, and the vicar never noticed what he put in his mouth anyway.

Carrying the flowers into the front parlor, Celia placed them on a low end table and looked critically around. She had polished the furniture herself that morning, and Jack, the yard boy, had given the worn carpet a vigorous beating. It was clean, at least, but if she'd had a month of Sundays to prepare the vicarage, it wouldn't have changed its shabby appearance. Regina would have to accept it as it was, Celia concluded practically.

The grandfather clock in the hallway chimed twice, and Celia hurried upstairs to change her dress. Regina was due in half an hour, and it would scarcely do to greet her in a rumpled gardening gown. She made her toilet swiftly and stood before the wavering mirror over her dresser, adjusting her starched cuffs. The middy blouse and dark blue skirt gave her more the appearance of a schoolgirl let off for the day than a young lady shortly to be married. The face that stared back at her was shaped delicately and blessed with a flawless complexion. That, along with a mass of silver-gilt curls, gave the impression that she was as fragile as a Dresden shepherdess. But Celia was no china doll. Her straightforward blue eyes and determined little chin showed there was more to her than chocolate-box prettiness. Circumstances had forced her to assume a great deal of responsibility in the running of the vicarage, and she displayed a fund of common sense for her age in all matters. Though many might be misled by her appearance, the vicar never made the mistake of supposing his daughter too fine for this world. Since his wife's death seven years ago, he had relied on Celia in every way imaginable. It was she who ordered the meals, made his appointments, then apologized nicely when he forgot them, saw that he ate properly, and bullied him into wearing his Wellingtons when it rained. Celia learned very quickly that her absentminded parent needed close mothering, and that her flustered housekeeper required careful watching. Now, at seventeen, she was a practical young woman, used to dealing with tradesmen and parishioners alike. The Dresden shepherdess was in charge of an entire flock, and she guarded them with her own brand of cheerful competence.

Hearing the clock strike the half hour, she gave one last pat to her curls and descended the stairs.

The stationmaster's wagon pulled into the drive of the vicarage and stopped abruptly to give Regina her first view of the gray, shingled manse that had lured her uncle away from Manchester. It was the idea of having a home of his own instead of rent-free lodgings in the city that had tempted Arthur Cressley to accept this living. His wife's passing also influenced his decision, and he decided that raising a daughter alone in a parish made up of common laborers was not an ideal situation.

Regina gazed at her uncle's dream house in astonishment while the driver grinned at her. "A beaut, ain't it?"

He was obviously quite proud of the edifice, and Regina didn't have the heart to denounce it for the monstrosity it was. A bizarre example of High Victorian Gothic, the vicarage sported innumerable gables and dormers, at least a dozen small stained glass windows, and such extraordinary wood trim that she wouldn't have found it unreasonable to see the Mad Hatter come dashing out. It was typical of Uncle Arthur, unworldly and fantastical.

Celia stepped outside the door just as Regina alighted. "Cousin Regina, I'm so happy to see you."

"Celia? It can't be. I don't believe it. Why, you're all grown up . . . and positively beautiful."

Expecting to see the same leggy child she remembered, Regina was startled by the change five years had made in her little cousin. The girl had an elegance and poise that was immediately apparent. Clear blue eyes smiled tentatively up at her, and Regina smiled back in delight. How lovely she was, Regina thought protectively.

Celia, too, was busy absorbing the unexpected. This Regina was older, dowdier than the smart young woman she remembered. It wasn't until the light brown eyes warmed and the firmly closed lips relaxed into a smile that Celia recognized her childhood friend and mentor. But why was she hidden under that drab green traveling suit and awful hat?

Making short shrift of the business of unloading Regina's luggage, the driver hauled the trunk up the staircase while Celia and Regina followed with some hatboxes.

"I hope you like this room, Regina. It's not the largest, but it has the prettiest view. You can't see the village street, but over there, through the trees, you can just get a glimpse of the castle. The Thwaits live there."

"You mean there isn't a prince or a princess, or even an enchanted frog living in it?"

Celia laughed. "Maybe there is a frog living there, after all, but I think he is quite an ordinary one. Here, let me help you unpack. Oh, this case just has papers in it."

"I'm afraid I can't escape my work completely, dear, although I am longing for a bit of country peace and quiet."

Celia was all sympathy. "Have you been over-working? You've certainly come to the right place for a rest. Things are rather dull in the village, to tell the truth. Not like in Manchester."

"I'm afraid Manchester is not exactly an abode of heavenly delight. Grantly's tranquility is just what I need."

That was a reasonable explanation for her sudden appearance after five years of excuses that she was too busy to make a brief train journey. Perhaps she simply needed a respite from the wars. Not many women could have achieved such distinction in a man's world, though Regina never referred to business affairs in her brief letters. It was Great-aunt Penelope who kept Celia informed about her cousin's financial conquests. Nevertheless, it must be fatiguing to keep up such a pace, and Celia insisted sweetly that Regina rest in the armchair while her clothes were being fitted into the small wardrobe.

"Do you mother everyone like this?" Regina couldn't help letting a certain amusement creep into her voice.

"Do you mean, am I always this commanding? I don't mean to be, but I'm afraid it's become a habit. Father won't move unless he's prodded, and Mrs. Gatchell needs constant organizing."

Regina watched Celia's deft movements as she arranged skirts on one side, blouses on the other. "Yet you look like a pink-and-white kitten."

"Disgusting, isn't it? I'm really very much like your mother. People are always fooled by Aunt Virginia with her fragile air and gentle demeanor."

"Fooled? What do you mean?"

"Oh, you know how she always gets her way in the end. As a matter of fact, I gather she handled your father so well he never realized he was being managed."

Regina was astounded. "Where did you get

such a ridiculous idea? My father ruled the household. He scarcely gave my mother room to breathe, much less consented to her requests."

Celia looked surprised. "That's not the way Aunt Virginia remembers it. Are you taken in as well? When your mother came to visit last year, she saw how much trouble I was having getting Father to take his heart medicine. She advised me to hide it for two days. By then he was frantic with worry, and I haven't had to coax him since. Now he takes it like a lamb. Doesn't that prove something?"

Regina smiled doubtfully. "Perhaps it proves that your father is more easily managed than my father was."

"But wasn't it clever of Aunt Virginia? You know, she told me that she misses Uncle Walter dreadfully."

"Believe me, Celia, Mother has never been happier than she is right now. Father was fearfully tyrannical, and she's delighted to be able to please herself."

"I see." Celia said nothing more, but she thought Regina was mistaken. Aunt Virginia did miss her husband, tyrannical or otherwise. Regina was a trifle overenthusiastic on the subject of independence, as she recalled, and independence can be lonely, Celia knew. She sincerely pitied her cousin's life of solitude in the big old Cressley mansion in Manchester.

When she finished hanging away Regina's clothes, she begged her to rest until teatime. "I'll call you the minute the table is laid," she promised.

Regina sank back into the chair gratefully. She was tired. How lucky that Celia had assumed that she had come down for a rest. But now that she was here, Regina felt a little hesitant about her rescue mission. It was not at all clear yet whether this rather forceful girl needed help. How accurate was Pen's information? Celia certainly didn't seem to be the type to be pushed into anything she didn't fancy, let alone an unwelcome marriage.

As for the story her mother had evidently told Celia about "managing" her husband, Regina dismissed it as the fabrication it was. Virginia had been in Bath so long under the influence of a lot of other old tabbies, she couldn't separate fact from dreams. What a shame Celia believed that nonsense! It was going to be useless to cite Mrs. Cressley as an example of the disaster that befalls girls who marry too young. But while Walter Cressley had been a household despot, it seemed that Celia's fiancé was a libertine. Regina thought that both types were a source of misery to their unfortunate wives.

Tea was a simple but ample repast, and Regina ate with surprising appetite while Celia chatted happily. "The Earl of Grantham is wonderfully generous about allowing Father the use of his library. That's where Father is now. He promised to be back for tea, but when he's at the priory he loses all track of time, for the library is full of rare volumes. Actually Lord Grantham says he is honored to have them put to use by a scholar like Father. Isn't that kind?"

"Lord Grantham? I think I knew his cousin once. An Alistair Debenham."

"But that's our Lord Grantham!" Celia crowed gleefully. "How exciting! I think he's come down from London, or will be here soon. Their Mabel told our Mrs. Gatchell so. He's such an important man, an MP no less, that I'm afraid the village rather keeps tabs on him. You'll see how it is in a place like this. No secrets at all."

Regina was overwhelmed by all this information. "But wasn't there a cousin or something? My Alistair wasn't really in line for the earldom," she protested feebly.

"*Your* Alistair! Oho!"

"Celia!" Regina's glance was quelling, and Celia smiled sheepishly.

"Yes. The cousin was killed in a hunting accident about eight years ago and that's when your Alistair succeeded. Or would you prefer that I call him *our* Alistair?" Celia said slyly. "If you knew him before, then he must have been madly in love with you. Everyone was, Aunt Penelope says. And you spurned them all for the sake of your career."

"Penelope is a fund of information, and most of it untrue. Your great-aunt has quite an imagination."

"Your great-aunt too," Celia reminded her.

But Regina needed no reminding that it was

due to that shared relationship that she was here now. Perhaps Pen had been equally theatrical in reporting Celia's affairs. The girl hadn't even mentioned her supposed engagement. Did it even exist?

"We're sure to be invited over to the priory while you are here. Lord Grantham gave Father this living, and we're really good friends. He lives with his sister, Miss Margaret. He's still a bachelor," Celia added significantly.

"I'm not interested," Regina said coolly, taking another cucumber sandwich and biting into it vigorously.

"Well, I admit he is rather old, but still handsome in his silver-haired way."

"Old? Silver-haired?" Regina exclaimed. "Why, he can't be more than forty!"

"You see, you are interested! You could still make him sit up and take notice, I'm sure."

"No matchmaking, Celia. I'm past all that sort of nonsense."

"How ridiculous! I don't believe any woman is ever past it! Why, old Mrs. Evans who's seventy-five and lives with her granddaughter has an admirer. He's only seventy."

Regina laughed. "So you love a romance? Then what about yourself? Is every boy in Grantly coming to call at the vicarage these days?"

Celia blushed. "Actually, there is someone . . . although nothing has been formally announced yet. But it's only a matter of days now."

"I see. And who is this . . . someone?"

Celia looked self-conscious for the first time. "He's wonderful, of course. His name is Tom Dawlish, and you'll meet him tonight. That is, I think he will come by tonight. He's a grand person, and I'm sure you'll like him."

Regina didn't press for more details, but it was clear that something was troubling her cousin. Most girls are only too eager to talk about their sweethearts, boring everyone with tiresome anecdotes proving their multiple perfections. Yet Celia was happy to discuss everything except her Tom. Perhaps Pen was right after all. It certainly bore looking into.

That evening the vicar filled in most of the gaps Celia failed to mention. The girl sat silent as her father rambled on about the merits of his future son-in-law. "The Dawlishes own some of the best farmland around here, and the squire is the master of the hunt. He's not a bookish man, I regret to say, but he always praises my sermons, especially the ones he sleeps through!" Mr. Cressley said with an impish smile.

It was clear that he, at least, was delighted with the match. But shouldn't he show some concern for the boy's character? The vicar might be deliberately blinding himself to the true state of affairs, as he did with anything that could interfere with his sublime isolation. It wasn't that he didn't care; he just couldn't cope with unpleasantness. He did admit that Tom was a little wild, but maintained that he was basically a good boy who would soon settle down when he married Celia.

"She'll keep him in line; she does me, you know." Uncle Arthur laughed to Regina.

Celia was very quiet during the meal, and Regina was not reassured. Something was troubling the girl, even if her father was unaware of it. Regina could understand her cousin's hesitation to disturb his illusions. A boy from such a background was not to be discarded lightly. It was with a great deal of curiosity that Regina awaited Tom's arrival that evening.

Dinner was well over, and the vicar secluded in his study, when a loud tattoo at the front door disrupted the quiet of the parlor, where Celia had been mending some stockings while Regina pored over a stack of papers from her briefcase.

Mrs. Gatchell answered the impatient knock, and Tom Dawlish made an impetuous entrance.

"Celia, love. This was the earliest I could get here. Did you miss me?"

Celia raised a shy face for his kiss, while Regina watched critically as Tom gave the girl an exuberant hug. So this was the rake. If only Pen could see. He was nothing more than a boy. His eyes were as blue as Celia's and just as guileless, and his tall, athletic body fairly radiated good health.

"I say, it's stuffy in here. Open a window, will you, Celia?"

At that moment he noticed the figure sitting at the table. Regina stared back at him just as frankly. He was a handsome boy, if somewhat young to be considering marriage.

The radiant look on Celia's face answered one question, at least. This was a love match, as far as her cousin was concerned. But until Regina could discover what was worrying the child, she was reserving judgment. Perhaps Tom sensed her coolness, for he was subdued as he acknowledged the introduction. Sitting awkwardly on the edge of the sofa, he cleared his throat self-consciously before offering a remark on the weather.

Celia was absolutely delighted that Tom had returned from London, and she questioned him eagerly about his trip. In a few minutes his discomfort was gone and he spoke amusingly on the pleasures of the city.

"But you might know," he concluded with a frown. "The minute I got back, the old man and I had a run-in." His eyes lit up for an instant. "Celia, I forgot to tell you, I bought an automobile. A crackerjack car with real silver spokes." He slumped dejectedly. "The Pater hates it. He threatened to dismantle it right there in the stables."

"You put an auto in the stables?" Celia asked.

"So? I moved Thunder first. His was the only stall large enough to hold it. You would have thought I personally gave the horse a chill," he sulked.

"Thunder is a great steeplechaser," Celia reminded him gently. "He's worth a lot of money."

"But the car's made by Daimler, and a darn close copy of the model that won the Paris–Bordeaux race this year. Believe me, it will someday be worth a good sight more than any old horse."

"I'm sure it will," Celia consoled him. "But you should have consulted your father for permission to use the stable before ousting poor Thunder. You know how he feels about his horse. Where is your automobile now?"

"In the hen house," he muttered dolefully.

Celia put a comforting arm around his dejected shoulders and patted him as though she would soothe an unhappy child.

"I hope you are not planning on any eggs for breakfast, Mr. Dawlish."

Tom looked across at Celia's cousin. Some sort of financial wizard, he remembered vaguely. "Don't you approve of cars?" he asked.

"I prefer them outside of chicken coops."

Tom's grievance caught what he thought was a sympathetic ear. "Don't I agree. Droppings all over the paint work could ruin it. Sea green too. Most cars are black," he felt obliged to explain.

"Did you choose the color yourself, or don't you ever get bilious?" Regina asked dryly.

"Oh, no. Tristam Barclay picked out the car. Green is his favorite color."

Regina felt rather green herself at that moment. Tristam Barclay! Good Lord, this was worse than anything she had imagined. "You are acquainted with Mr. Barclay?" she queried faintly.

"He's my best friend," was the boastful answer. "I'm always going up to London with him. His country place is near the Grange, and I daresay

I'm there more than I'm at home. Tristam's a swell chap."

"Indeed."

"I can see you are surprised, Miss Cressley," Tom said with a naive smile. "What would a fellow like Barclay want with a clod like me? But truly, we have lots in common."

"Not everything, I hope, Mr. Dawlish."

Tom was aware of the implied criticism in Regina's tone, but happily he was in ignorance of the reason behind it. "Some people don't approve of him, I know. But that just shows how hopelessly out of date they are. Poets are not all feckless creatures. Isn't that right, Celia?"

Celia gave a rather noncommittal smile.

"She really hasn't seen that much of him," Tom hastened to explain. "But he's a capital writer. I can hardly understand half of what he says. But once Celia gets to know him like I do, she'll be just as impressed. The ladies in London think he's fascinating."

"Some gentlemen too," Regina said under her breath.

"Never you fear, Miss Cressley," Tom went on. "Wait till you meet Tristam, then you'll forget about all those lies people circulate about him. They are just jealous of his superior talent."

"I'm looking forward to the experience."

Regina's mind was whirling. No wonder Pen had written that panicked request. Bad company was a rather mild description of what Tom had fallen into. It certainly explained why the squire was so anxious to marry off his young son to the vicar's daughter, as if purity stood a chance against that evil influence. Barclay's crowd was a byword in the country, his reputation almost as tarnished as Oscar Wilde's. Yet the boy seemed nice enough, even innocent. But if he was Tristam Barclay's best friend—and Regina hoped it was mostly wishful thinking on Tom's part—then how long before he, too, was corrupted? This situation called for careful handling.

Gathering her papers together, Regina left the two young people with the excuse that she had to consult the vicar about one of her business problems. Celia gave her a disbelieving look, but when Tom suggested a stroll in the garden, she sighed blissfully and promptly forgot about her cousin.

Regina knocked once, then walked into the study. The vicar peered at her from over the rim of his spectacles, his faded blue eyes only mildly curious at his niece's abrupt entry. He recognized the look of battle in her eyes, as his brother Walter, too, had that pugnacious manner when he was angry. Regina, it appeared, had bothersome matters on her mind. But the vicar was skilled at turning off any unpleasantness.

His niece found him maddeningly obtuse. "But I tell you," she repeated, fast losing her patience, "Tristam Barclay as a rival for Tom's affection is sure to bring Celia nothing but unhappiness. Even in Manchester his licentious ways are spoken of. As for his claim to be a poet, his *Odes to Elinor* was just a piece of lewdness and written in

37

macaronics, at that. Just think, Uncle, if she marries Tom, Barclay will be a frequent visitor in her house, and she will be exposed to all sorts of improper conversation. Perhaps it would go no farther, but who can say with one so depraved."

"Grantly is hardly Sodom and Gomorrah." The vicar raised bland eyes to see his niece throw up her hands in exasperation.

"How would you know? If vice and corruption were right under your nose, you wouldn't recognize them. Grantly could be a den of opium smokers, but as long as you have your head buried in some Bible or other, you would never notice."

"There is only one Bible that I know of, unless you are referring to the Koran or one of the Hindu scriptures."

"Uncle, I'm talking about Tristam Barclay."

"Ah, yes, I remember. It's on the bottom shelf. A copy of the Veda. These sutras deal with all sorts of things. Cows, for instance. Cows are not given much attention by the Anglican church. I'm rather fond of cows. Gentle, unassuming creatures. I wonder if they say anything about horses also?"

Regina took a deep breath. "Then you won't do anything about Celia's problem?"

"But I don't see any problem, my dear. Celia is quite happy. Are you sure you really understand the situation? Oh, here it is . . . the sacred cow. Horses must be in the next chapter."

Temporarily defeated, Regina left her uncle to

his investigation into the importance of equines in India, but she intended to have a long talk with Celia. The poor child had no one else to advise her; even Aunt Pen was unavailable in her hour of need. Regina knew now that her decision to come to Grantly was inspired. As no one else would, it was left to her to dissuade Celia from rushing into something she might regret the rest of her life.

CHAPTER THREE

"So there's no possibility of a women's suffrage bill this session." Miss Margaret Debenham shook her head with gloomy satisfaction. "It is thirty years since the movement began, and we are no closer to passage today. Your aunt Penelope must be as disheartened as I am." She spoke with the authority of one who understands the workings of Providence.

Miss Margaret was much as Regina had expected. A good fifteen years older than her brother, she occupied herself with the topic of suffrage by writing long letters to *The Times* and hostessing the more liberal members of Parliament, either at Grantham Priory or the Debenham townhouse in London. Showing an interest in the women's movement had brought her her brother's approbation without the least inconvenience, as Margaret left the more unpleasant work to others. Still, she perceived herself as the heroine of a long-fought battle, struggling valiantly against the oppression of a male-dominated world.

Regina found this attitude more than a little bogus and wondered acidly what Aunt Pen would say if she heard this harangue. But she listened to her hostess's political chatter with her usual good-mannered calm, all the while very conscious of the silent man next to her.

The invitation to tea at the priory had been given a great deal of attention at the vicarage. Evidently a summons to the Great House was a rare and valued treat, despite Celia's claims of friendship with Lord Grantham. Having already promised to play tennis at the castle with Tom and a group of young people, Celia was distressed at having to decline. She even considered begging off from tennis, but Regina dissuaded her. It would hardly be honorable to cancel her engagement because a more flattering invitation had been extended at the last moment.

"You're right, of course. But what a shame I can't come with you and Papa!"

Then, in the end, Regina had gone alone. Mr. Cressley had to attend a meeting of the board of trustees of the local orphanage. "When I'm not there, they vote the most stringent economies, and the poor children have to subsist on potato soup," her uncle apologized.

"Don't fret, Uncle. The orphans needn't go hungry for my sake."

Regina had no intention of crying off. She was anxious to meet Miss Margaret, she told Celia, but not especially curious to see what the years had done to Alistair, she told herself. He was probably fat as well as silver-haired by now. Disillusionment was, after all, a fitting end to the callow passions of puppy love, and Regina braced herself for the worst.

But as the butler ushered her into Grantham Priory, she had to make a quick reevaluation. Celia's description was far from accurate and totally unlike the distinguished man striding across the drawing room to greet her. For a moment it was almost like seeing a ghost from the past, but as he drew closer, she could discern the silver at his temples and the fine network of wrinkles around his piercing gray eyes. No doubt he had aged, but only to grow more attractive, she allowed with surprise.

The years had treated him lightly, and Regina wished the same could be said for herself. What was considered maturity in a man was not nearly so flattering in a woman. Then, remembering her particular status in this world and how little looks mattered to it, Regina greeted the earl formally, ignoring his strongly raised brows as his eyes took in her brown tweed walking suit. Next to Miss Margaret's mauve silk tea gown, it did seem terribly out of place in a drawing room. Nevertheless, she was Regina Cressley and that fact required no further embellishment.

The Earl of Grantham made the necessary introductions, with only a passing reference to having met Miss Cressley a dozen years before in London. Since that was a rather casual explanation for a more than casual relationship, Regina admitted to a stab of resentment. Then, in all fairness, she realized how uncomfortable it would be to discuss what was, after all, best forgotten.

Taking a seat near her hostess, Regina examined the room with interest. It was enormous and filled with priceless treasures. She recognized a couple of Van Dycks, and a Constable hanging beside a Louis XIV cabinet. The walls were covered with blue silk above the walnut wainscoting, and although Regina was no expert on furnishings, she did note that the few examples of French gilt among the more massive pieces added a touch of lightness and charm to the formal grandeur.

Conversation began with the normal social formulas: a discussion of the weather, the dismal state of the British railroad system, and a brief diatribe on scandal-mongering newssheets. Once Miss Margaret was launched on her favorite theme, it became more of a monologue, and Regina withdrew from the conversation to help herself to the lavish assortment of sandwiches and cakes.

"I think it is appalling that the question of the vote for women should be a cause for laughter in the House of Lords. Crude jokes about petticoat government cannot be tolerated. Something should be done about it," Margaret stated.

"And what do you suggest, Miss Cressley?" came a lazy, masculine voice.

The earl's question took Regina by surprise, since his sister's speech was no more than empty rhetoric. But Regina was well schooled on the topic of suffrage. "I think it's time for a nationwide petition," she answered smartly, after only the barest of pauses. "The government could not ignore ten thousand signatures."

"How would you get them? Go door to door?" Grantham asked, a hint of laughter in his voice.

"Of course not," Margaret interrupted. "The idea is repugnant to every womanly instinct."

Attacked on both sides now, Regina could only defend herself, and Aunt Pen's sentiments as well. "A door to door solicitation would be terribly inefficient. Rallies, large open-air rallies, would be the answer. You'd draw the people who are sympathetic and have them sign the petitions. Perhaps ten thousand is a little optimistic, but whatever the number, it would be a good tactic. Until women exert themselves in their own behalf, their pleas to be taken seriously will fall on deaf ears. No victories are won without a struggle."

Miss Margaret smiled condescendingly. "Your sentiments are mine exactly, Miss Cressley. But I'm afraid your political . . . naiveté, dare I say, has led you to an error in judgment. Rallies, particularly out-of-doors, attract the most vulgar crowds. Their main delight seems to be heckling and laughing at the women. No, the best method is the one that has achieved so much in the past: quiet, well-bred meetings with men of influence."

"But you yourself admit that there has been no progress in years. Apparently these quiet, well-bred meetings are not as effective as you think. It is time now for more vigorous strategies." Regina's comments showed rather more awareness of the situation than either her great-aunt or her secretary would have credited.

Margaret's smile had grown a little fixed by now. "Are you offering to organize a rally here in Grantly?" she asked, raising one rather heavy eyebrow.

"Of course not. But if you would care to, I'd be happy to assist." The last was thrown in to wipe that supercilious look off her hostess's face.

But Miss Debenham was not beaten so easily. "You see, even you draw back when faced with such a wild scheme. Public discussions of women's rights would do more harm than good. We would appear mannish and unfeminine. That only gives fuel to our detractors, who claim that education and the vote will unfit women for their traditional roles as wives and mothers. No, Miss Cressley, that we do not want. To compete with men would be unseemly. Our objective is to be allowed some voice in conducting our affairs, not to try and run things ourselves." Margaret leaned back, satisfied that she had silenced all opposition.

Regina was quite ready to take issue with her, but Lord Grantham swiftly intervened. "Not compete? Ridiculous! You've been bullying me successfully for forty years, Margaret. And I've never come close to winning an argument yet."

"I wish you wouldn't talk nonsense, Alistair. Miss Cressley will get quite the wrong impression."

"Then I retract my statement. You see, Miss Cressley, how she rules me?" He smiled.

But Margaret was not best pleased with such jokes and sent him an angry glance.

Regina also ignored the earl's attempt to smooth over what had become a rather heated discussion. "Then you think we women should sit back and wait for the world to recognize our innate ability, or should I say, nobility? It will be a long wait, I'll wager."

Margaret stared haughtily at this presumptuous woman. Miss Cressley was typical of the extremists who dared push themselves into spheres where females had no right to be. "The queen does not approve of the 'new woman.' She feels there has been quite enough change already."

"Yet the queen herself is an example, a potent example, of what strength and leadership a woman is capable," Regina said. "And how superior a monarch she has been to those kings who preceded her."

Lord Grantham gave a short laugh. "She's got you there, Margaret! And I'm afraid you're found out. Miss Cressley sees that, despite your talk of votes for women, you're quite content with the status quo."

"I am not against Miss Cressley's principles, Alistair. I am only questioning her methods. The petition is quite a good idea, but the movement must maintain its dignity. There can be no suggestion of radicalism. After all, we are not fishwives, screaming down the opposition."

"Actually, I think all women should sign the petition; women from every corner of Great Britain, from every walk of life, even fishwives. Now that would be effective, don't you think?" Regina looked straight at her hostess.

"Women sign the petition? My dear Miss Cressley, how futile. Parliament will not listen to us. It must be the men who sign it. After all, they are the ones who vote."

Regina looked at this supposedly enlightened leader of the suffrage movement in sad disillusion. No wonder Aunt Pen claimed it was an uphill battle. With influential women like Margaret Debenham unwilling to risk their genteel reputations, there was little hope for the Cause. Even Lord Grantham must find his sister's attitudes more of a hindrance than a help. His aid to the movement was, at least, constructive, if not especially successful, according to Celia.

"This is quite a notion you have, Miss Cressley," he commented. "Parliament is full of married men who probably pay more attention to their wives' opinions than they care to admit. It might even work."

The earl's eyes were twinkling at her, and Regina decided he was having a little joke at her expense. Stiffly, she explained, "I'm not suggesting that men be badgered into supporting the Cause, my lord, but that the government may be convinced by a show of numbers."

"Very likely," Margaret concluded tepidly, resolved to end this unproductive discussion. She would speak to Alistair later about his disloyal levity. "I'm so sorry that Miss Celia Cressley could not join us this afternoon. Such a sweet girl."

"She was sorry to decline, but she had promised to go to a tennis party at the castle."

"Ah, yes. The Thwaits." Miss Margaret dismissed them as beneath consideration. "I hear the annual church fête is to be held at the castle, after all. I don't approve with the duke so recently deceased. Not that the Thwaits are any connection of his, but it would be a mark of good taste if such frivolities were postponed for a year or two. It was his custom, of course, to sponsor the fête, though why the Thwaits should succeed to the duke's privileges as well as his home remains a mystery to me."

"Are they his heirs?" Regina asked in all innocence.

"Not at all," was the firm reply. "They bought the castle. A totally presumptuous move, as Mrs. Thwait is the daughter of a common merchant. Her husband works in the city too. Certainly not the kind of people the duke would have chosen to sell to, but at the time his financial position was desperate. I don't receive them, but not everyone is so particular."

Regina defended Celia's friendship with a member of the lower classes. "My cousin says they are quite charitable."

"Of course they are," Miss Margaret said tartly. "They are trying to buy acceptance. And Jeremy Thwait can afford to do so on a grand scale. I think it is unfortunate that the church lends itself to that sort of thing."

Regina glossed over the insult to her uncle Arthur's integrity because another, more startling revelation had come out of Margaret's snide comments. This was the first time Regina was made aware that the Mr. Thwait who lived in the castle was the same Jeremy Thwait who had made an offer on John Lassiter's shares. How odd that she hadn't made the connection before, though there had been other things on her mind at the time. Still, to be so oblivious of the very name that Colonel Pucey was waving about like a banner only emphasized just how engrossed Regina was with Celia's problems. Not that the matter of Jeremy Thwait was any more than an empty threat, but it did seem propitious that her impulsive journey from Manchester would bring her right into the enemy's camp, so to speak. Deep in her musing, Regina only caught the end of Margaret's words.

". . . so we are quite pleased about Celia and Tom Dawlish. He is such a charming boy. Your cousin is very fortunate."

Regina stared at her hostess in annoyance. There was no match as yet, not even a formal announcement, but it seemed that everyone was certain of the outcome. "She is terribly young," Regina stated firmly. "Too young, in my opinion, to think of marriage."

"Do you think so? But then we middle-aged

people have forgotten what it means to be eager and in love."

The earl smiled benignly, but his eyes held a challenge. "I don't think most of us have forgotten, do you, Miss Cressley?"

"I never look back," Regina responded. "Memory can play foolish tricks. Middle-aged people tend to glorify their past, a more flattering view that way."

"I cannot believe you would fall into that trap, Miss Cressley. Your sensible nature indicates a far more realistic approach. But I wonder," he mused. "Have you never played the game of what might have been?"

"Never," Regina said coolly.

Margaret was baffled by the curious exchange between her brother and this forward woman, but she assumed Alistair found her as incomprehensible as she did herself. Happily, the visit was over and Margaret need not worry herself further. Her farewell to Miss Cressley was a trifle stiff.

"Allow me to drive you back in the trap," Grantham offered.

"That is not necessary," Regina declined. "I enjoy a country walk."

"Even better. I'm in need of a bit of exercise after so many months in London. A walk sounds like a fine idea."

Regina had no recourse but to accept, as she could think of no way to refuse without sounding churlish. But she maintained a stubborn silence all the way down the flagstone path to the road.

The last thing she wanted was a private conversation with the Earl of Grantham. He was not nearly as charming as he used to be.

Twelve years before, when he was still plain Mr. Debenham, he had been a most devoted suitor during her one and only season in London. She had enjoyed his company and been stimulated by the electric attraction between them. Their conversation held a certain intellectual acerbity, and he had been the one young man Regina could neither condescend to nor ignore. But that was a lifetime ago.

"Twelve years is a long time, Regina."

She looked up quickly. He still had the uncanny ability to read her mind, though naturally they both would be thinking of the past right now, she reminded herself. "Twelve years and five days to be exact. It was the day after Papa's funeral. I could never forget."

"Then why pretend you did? Is youth so long gone that you can't recognize an old flame?"

"Old flame? That is not how you introduced me to your sister. A mere acquaintance was more like it, or did I miss something?"

"Now that I know how you feel about the subject, you can be sure that the next time you see Margaret, she will be fully cognizant of our abortive affair."

"It was never an affair," Regina denied heatedly.

"My mistake. Shall I refer to myself as a rejected suitor?"

"You can wear a placard for all I care, though I don't see the need to resurrect a dead issue."

"It is not at all dead when you flash your eyes at me like that."

"If, by any chance, you imagine that I came to see you today, let me dispel the notion. It was your sister I wanted to meet. My aunt Pen has mentioned her frequently."

"So you want to forget about the past."

"I already have."

"Yet you just stated that you would never forget. Ever the paradox of mind and nature, eh, Ginny?"

"Please don't call me Ginny."

"Sorry. I forgot you are now the important Miss Cressley. Yet I can't help preferring my sweet Ginny."

"I was never sweet."

"Endearing then. I found it rather charming when you climbed up on your soapbox and spouted the principles of emancipation at me. But I was always able to bring you down with kisses, remember?"

Regina remembered only too well. "The very reason I refused your offer of marriage. You used brute force when logic failed, and I found it intolerable."

"You liked it."

Regina increased her stride, an expression of prim disapproval marking her face. "I can find my way home from here, Lord Grantham. There is no need to inconvenience yourself further."

"I have no intention of abandoning you to the perils of this footpath. If you were to fall, you might not be found for ten minutes at least."

"How considerate of you, my lord. But the vicarage is only a few steps away, and I daresay, once I am out of your sight, I shall come to no further harm."

"My dear girl," he protested with a droll smile, "I didn't mean to offend you. It's just that, despite your dreadfully intimidating suit, I can't help feeling a certain admiration."

"That's a backhanded compliment if I ever heard one."

"Not at all. It's just that I am able to penetrate your disguise. You may hide that glorious hair in a bird's nest and try to conceal what is still a perfectly good figure, but underneath is the Ginny I remember." He took her arm in a careless hold and continued their passage down the winding lane.

What a farrago of tomfoolery this was, Regina fumed. "Surely your grudge should have died a natural death by now, but I see that time has only increased your sense of pique. Let us hope this double-edged flattery assuages your wounded vanity."

"That is a very interesting theory, Regina, but unfortunately, in my case, untrue. I hate to disappoint you by admitting that I have not been nursing a grudge all these years. The truth is, when you likened marriage to me as a form of life-long suffocation, I realized that for you, it might be.

No, I harbor no ill will; I'm merely curious. I can't help wondering why the drastic change in you."

"I grew up, Lord Grantham. You would do well to follow my example and not act the ageless coxcomb."

"Then you consider us both over the hill. Too bad. If my calculations are correct, you cannot be much over thirty, yet you pretend to impending senility."

"Not quite. I've just discarded all that fashionable nonsense about clothes."

"Have you considered sack cloth and ashes?"

"No need to be sarcastic. It's very simple. As I want to be taken seriously, I must make the men with whom I work forget I am a woman."

"A hopeless task."

Regina smiled coolly. "Perhaps. At any rate, sensible clothes show a sensible person. Frills and ribbons create the impression that I require pampering and protecting. Very pleasant, of course, but destructive of respect. And respect is a rarer and more valuable commodity than pretty speeches and empty flattery."

"I hope you are not dismissing my efforts for female enfranchisement as mere pampering and protecting."

"Oh, I forgot. You are for women's suffrage. My aunt Pen would adore you."

"And you?"

"You have my respect for espousing such an unpopular and unrewarding cause."

"Respect. A tepid sort of feeling. I was hoping

for something a little warmer. After all, I do deserve a boon for giving your uncle this church. Of course, I didn't expect it would take you five years to show up, or I might have thought twice about it."

"You gave Uncle Arthur this living for my sake? How ridiculous! I don't believe it. I'm sure he is well qualified for his position."

"He is. But then, so were others."

Regina looked at him doubtfully. "A lingering attachment?" she asked.

"Let us say, a sentimental gesture."

"I find that hard to believe. You are the least sentimental person I know."

"You malign me, Ginny. Wasn't I out to charm you all afternoon?"

Regina laughed at this absurdity, knowing full well he meant not a word of it. "Are you so lacking in female adulation that I must add my name to the list of your admirers? Come, come, my lord. I'll wager you're chased by petticoats the length and breadth of England."

"You flatter me, Miss Cressley. I am, as you say, but an aging coxcomb."

"Ageless," she corrected. "But you called me worse. Impending senility, indeed."

"I recant," he smiled. "You are far too sharp for that appellation."

They were falling into an easy camaraderie that belied the caustic overtones of their conversation. Regina rather enjoyed it, though she wouldn't give Lord Grantham the satisfaction of admitting it. He was far too sure of himself as it was.

"So tell me, what brings you to Grantly, Ginny? Now that I know it wasn't to see me again, there must be another equally pressing reason to prod you out of your office."

"Why should there be any reason?" she asked cautiously.

"Your uncle has been here for five years, yet this is your first visit. I can only conclude it has something to do with your cousin's wedding plans. You certainly flew into the boughs when Margaret mentioned it."

"I certainly did not. It's just that everyone seems to be taking it for granted."

"And now that you are here, the odds have changed."

"Nonsense. I simply want to see Celia happy."

"As it coincides with your concept of happiness. You forget, I know that facet of your character very well."

"You've just proved you don't know me at all. I only think Celia is too young to know her own mind. Marriage is so final."

"It is not a sentence to be hanged, Regina. Some people actually like it."

She glanced up at him pertly. "Is that why you've avoided the state all these years? Because you like the idea so well?"

The earl turned her around to face him and smiled dangerously into her eyes. "Be careful what you suggest, Regina. I might take you up on your offer."

Cursed man! She pulled herself out of his arms and stalked on. As if Miss Regina Cressley had any intention of making a play for him. She'd show him in no uncertain terms that he had no effect on her whatsoever.

"Regina." He touched her arm and she jumped. "You dropped your handkerchief. No need to glare at me like that. It's still in one piece. And so are you."

"No thanks to you."

"My dear girl, I do believe you are afraid."

"Only cautious. You are a crusty old bachelor with a deplorable tendency to tease."

"And you cannot separate fact from fiction."

"You have taken far too much license based on too little foundation," Regina said emphatically. "Our past association does not entitle you to treat me in such a fashion. We are strangers now, Lord Grantham."

"Never that, Ginny." He bent his head close to her face, and Regina instinctively leaned toward him. "I think we've arrived at the vicarage," he said softly.

Regina gathered her wits. "So we have. Thank you, my lord. It has been a very instructive afternoon."

"My pleasure, Miss Cressley." He doffed his hat and opened the gate for her. "Please give my regards to the vicar."

CHAPTER FOUR

After three whole days at Grantly, Regina had achieved absolutely nothing. A letter from her secretary reminded her that this prolonged absence was achieving no results in Manchester either. In fact, Dottie was full of complaints that too much responsibility was falling on her own shoulders, concluding with a blatant attempt to bully Regina into returning to the office.

. . . I always said you placed too much trust in John Lassiter. The man flows with the tide. When Colonel Pucey mentioned Jeremy Thwait, I knew it meant trouble. The two are thick as thieves, by all accounts, and with much the same purpose. You should return at once, for the office is full of rumors, and your absence is taken as proof that something is up.

It's no secret that Lassiter wants to sell out, but are you sure he doesn't mean to sell you out as well? He's off to Italy, for his health he says. But I think it's suspicious. When are you coming home?

Faithfully yours,
Dorothy Hodgekiss

This news was disturbing, but not the catastrophe Dottie made it. John Lassiter would not let himself be used by the colonel or any of his nefarious friends, no matter how suspicious this sudden trip of his seemed. He was probably just stringing Pucey along for the fun of it. The two had always been at loggerheads, and John's wry sense of humor was ever a source of irritation to the unimaginative colonel. No, Dottie was just overexcited at being left on her own. John would never consider selling out behind her back when he was the one who put her on top to begin with. Nevertheless, Regina did wish he had let her know he was leaving the country. She could have completed the sale before he left and squashed these rumors at the outset. They were Pucey's doing, no doubt.

The colonel had never forgiven Regina for wresting control of Cressley Limited away from him and was not above using Jeremy Thwait to get it back. But that was all talk and little promise. John Lassiter would never allow it to happen. Regina ordered Dottie to send a cable off to him immediately. Once the formalities of the sale were completed, it would put an end to the colonel's troublemaking.

The sleepy little village of Grantly was proving far more absorbing than Regina could have imagined. But the frustration of not being able to control events, for once in her life, was unsettling. As long as Lord Grantham stayed out of reach, Regina could not give him the setdown he deserved.

Worse, Celia had announced only this morning that her engagement to Tom Dawlish was to be made official at last.

Unfortunately Celia seemed determined on what her cousin foresaw as a disastrous marriage. The girl still had said nothing of the doubts she had expressed to Aunt Pen, and as the engagement party was to be held at the Grange the next night, there was no time to be lost. After that official announcement, things would be more difficult to arrange . . . or disarrange.

Celia had caught Regina's fancy. Far from being a dull little girl, the seventeen-year-old showed a maturity and intelligence that would be wasted in a marriage to a thoughtless, selfish young man. Celia had great potential, and Regina had resolved that the girl should have every opportunity of education and time to discover and develop her capabilities.

As soon as Mrs. Gatchell took her curious presence from the room, Regina began boldly enough over the tea table. "Celia, may I be utterly frank with you?"

Celia was startled by the intensity of Regina's expression, but not surprised. With a motherly solicitude that might have been funny if Regina had been in a mood to appreciate it, Celia offered encouragement. "Of course! I knew there must be something wrong when you arrived in Grantly so suddenly. Believe me, Father and I are ready to help you in any way we can."

"What?" Regina was unaware that her own

troubled thoughts sometimes showed on her face. She would have been more astounded if she knew the conclusions Celia had drawn after her visit to Grantham Priory. The younger Miss Cressley was every bit as astute as her older cousin, even more so when it came to human nature. Celia saw the look on Lord Grantham's face when he escorted Regina home, and she knew her cousin was not indifferent to him either, no matter how much she protested. But unlike Regina, Celia was not one to charge in uninvited. She had her own way of achieving results, thanks to Aunt Virginia.

Regina was quick to disabuse her cousin of the notion that she required help, but she was touched by the thought nonetheless. "It is not any problem of mine that needs solving, Celia dear, but your own."

Celia wrinkled up her nose in perplexity. "What can you mean?"

"It's not too late. You can still extricate yourself from this . . . engagement. I'll stand behind you all the way."

"What has given you the idea that I want to cry off? Why, I have cared for Tom since we moved here five years ago."

"At twelve one frequently forms attachments that are unsuitable," Regina said dryly.

Two spots of color glowed alarmingly in Celia's pale cheeks, and Regina realized too late that her blunt words had been a gross tactical error. Celia couldn't be bludgeoned into confessing her misgivings; they would have to be coaxed out of her, carefully and with great delicacy. No, Regina had only succeeded in offending her.

"If you are suggesting that I am too young to know my own mind, I would like to remind you that you can hardly be an authority on the situation. I love Tom, and if my father finds the match suitable, you need not concern yourself."

Regina had been put very firmly in her place. Nevertheless she was not one to abandon a position lightly. She also knew that the best defense is an attack, preferably on an undefended flank. "You may be sure of your own feelings, but what of Tom's? His behavior to you borders on the neglectful, my dear. And if one cannot count on a man's devotion before the wedding, it is quite useless to expect things to improve later on. Rather the reverse." Regina spoke with a calm she was far from feeling. She was being cruel, she knew, but it was better for Celia to face the truth than to suffer a lifetime of regret.

Celia was now pale instead of flushed, and she was silent for a moment, as if gathering her resolution. "Neglectful, Regina? That is unfair. He has been taken up with . . . other things. Besides, I don't expect him to dangle after me like some lovesick swain in a book," she finished with an effort.

Regina raised one eyebrow. "Really? I think Tom Dawlish is a nice enough boy, but a boy nonetheless. He is no more ready to settle down to marriage than his friend, Tristam Barclay." Regina dropped Barclay's name with serious intent and waited for Celia's reaction.

"Oh, Barclay! Tom is a little too . . . that is, Squire Dawlish dislikes him, but that is just his prejudice, Tom says. Mr. Barclay is a poet and has written a play in verse that Tom says is very amusing. You can see why the squire, who is dreadfully old-fashioned, is against him. But, Regina, I thought you were too sophisticated to condemn someone because they wear long hair and velvet collars!" Celia spoke very fast and seemed to be appealing to her companion for understanding.

Regina took her hand. "Dear child, Tom is fascinated by that man. And Barclay is no friend of yours."

Celia's sigh was heartbreakingly touching, and she seemed to have trouble raising her eyes from the slender hand resting on her own. "I should have known I couldn't fool you for long, Regina. I wrote to Aunt Pen, but then I felt so silly about it afterwards. How ridiculous," she said tremulously, "to be jealous of a man. But I can't help it. If it were another woman, I might be able to cope. As it is . . . Tom quotes him at me until I think I could scream." She smiled wanly. "I am not one of those possessive females who demand that their sweethearts give up all their friends and usual pleasures. But I am right, aren't I? Mr. Barclay is a bad influence on Tom."

Regina looked at Celia narrowly. No, she was too innocent to know what she had implied. "You are absolutely right. Barclay is shallow and malicious, and a terrible poet to boot! But we will never convince Tom of that by telling him so. Your fiancé will have to discover his friend's character for himself. Even if Tom loves you, he needs time to grow up. And it wouldn't hurt for you to wait. Seventeen is too young for such a commitment."

Celia looked remarkably stubborn. "No, no. I don't see that."

"Well, why not postpone the announcement? That would give you both time to discover if your attachment is real. In the meantime, come live with me. We could spend the autumn in Europe. I've always wanted to travel, and it would be delightful with you for company."

"Oh, Cousin Regina, how kind you are! But you are wrong. After all, you've barely spoken to Tom; you don't do him justice. Because I am only seventeen you assume I am just a little silly. But I am grown up in all the ways that matter. I have been taking care of Father for ages, and I know how to run a house. I will be a good wife to Tom!"

"Celia, Celia. You are much too good for Tom. Despite all romances to the contrary, dashing young men make execrable husbands and worse fathers."

"Please, I cannot listen to you when you speak against Tom."

There was so much dignity in Celia's reproach that Regina felt a qualm at what she was doing. Was she right in interfering? "Your loyalty is commendable. Just let me say that marriage is a very serious business. It is the rest of your life. Don't be in a hurry to make what might be a tragic mistake. Please, think about what you are doing!"

Celia looked distressed. "Haven't you ever been in love, Regina? When you're in love you don't have to think. You know."

Regina almost laughed out loud at this piece of romantic claptrap that only showed how naive Celia was. Suppressing the amusement that would have wounded the girl's feelings, she answered seriously, "No one escapes that malady. Luckily it is not a permanent condition, even if one thinks so at the time."

"You are very cynical. I'm sorry if you were hurt once."

"Are you supposing that I loved and lost? You are quite mistaken, child. Fortunately I know myself too well. I prefer freedom even at the cost of a heart-stirring, though temporary, rapture. And I have met many a woman who wished that she had chosen as I did. But I am not advocating my sort of life for you. I'm only offering you any support you need, moral and financial, so that you can choose freely what you really want. If you are marrying Tom to escape into a larger and more interesting world than your father's vicarage, don't. Come with me to Manchester instead. There are many more men in the world than can be met in Grantly."

"Thank you, but no. I want to marry Tom. And I think I can learn to cope with Mr. Barclay.

Talking to you has made me feel so much better."

That was not the reaction for which Regina had hoped, but it was some consolation if it eased Celia's worries. "If you should change your mind, remember that my offer still holds."

Celia kissed Regina on the cheek. "I hope this doesn't mean that you will disappear for another five years."

"Oh, Celia. I do feel guilty. I've neglected you so abominably! Indeed, I won't go away. I'll even stay in Grantly a little longer, if I may?"

"Of course. You know we want you to stay just as long as you possibly can."

So it was settled. If Regina still hoped that their discussion might bear fruit, outwardly she was resigned to the approaching nuptials.

The Grange was a mellow, brick dwelling dating from the time of Queen Anne. Succeeding generations of Dawlishes were conservative enough to think well of their home and leave it in all its original and sturdy grace. The recent addition of drains, water closets, and a large, patented stove in the kitchen, plus a profusion of gaslights, had improved its comfort without altering its appearance. Indeed, the old house was as warmly welcoming as the squire and his wife were when the three from the vicarage arrived. They had walked over in the soft twilight while the scent of June roses lay heavy in the hedge-lined lane.

Regina, disapproving as she was of this engagement party, was touched by the genuine affection with which the Dawlishes greeted Celia and her father. Mrs. Dawlish, a faded blonde, rather given to flowing draperies that tangled precariously around her feet, twittered gently at Celia's young beauty.

"Isn't she exquisite, John? Bless you, how John and I have missed having a daughter since Agatha and her husband have been in India. Dear Vicar, you will share Celia with us, won't you? You must consider the Grange your other home, my dear! We expect to see a great deal of you before the wedding."

The squire shook hands heartily with Mr. Cressley and pinched Celia on the cheek. "Well, well, Puss!" he smiled. "Tom's a lucky dog, and his mother and I know it."

Celia blushed and blushed again, overwhelmed, but pleased and flattered as well. Even Regina could see no fault in either the Dawlishes' home or manners. But Celia was marrying Tom, not his parents.

Tom's welcome was a touch too offhand for Regina's taste as he hurried to introduce Miss Cressley to his friend, Tristam Barclay.

Regina stared back as two protuberant brown eyes looked her over appraisingly. The man's full red lips were partially hidden by a particularly formidable moustache, waxed and curled into Mephistophelean twists. His rather dissipated face topped a youthfully slight body clothed in exaggerated elegance.

"Miss Cressley, delighted to meet you at last."

Barclay's voice was a pleasing baritone, his accent charmingly Oxonian, but his extravagantly cut dinner jacket betrayed a heavy touch of the bohemian in the widening of the lapels and the velvet cuffs on the sleeve. There was even a ruby stickpin showing through the cascade of ruffles on his shirt-front.

Regina decided to be dismissively cool to this pretentious fellow. "At last, Mr. Barclay?" she queried with lukewarm interest.

"Why, yes. We have at least one friend in common . . . someone who has spoken of you often—and in the highest terms."

He stood smiling at her, one hand smoothing his moustache, waiting to see if the austere Miss Cressley had enough feminine curiosity to ask the obvious question.

"One has so many acquaintances," Regina murmured.

Her complete disinterest was a clear indication of just what she thought of any friend they might have in common, and Barclay had to admit to a grudging admiration for her deliberate indifference. Used to fawning tributes, he found it refreshing to find someone so completely unimpressed with him. That didn't mean that Miss Cressley would escape unscathed. His eyes shone maliciously.

"Yes," he drawled, "you are very much as he reported . . . an original."

Regina's tone held a touch of malice also. "How

interesting. Then I'm sure our mutual acquaintance finds you just as . . . unusual."

Barclay threw back his head and gave a full-throated laugh. Miss Cressley was a formidable opponent, and despite the setdown she had just inflicted, he enjoyed the verbal sparring with her. It wasn't often he found someone worthy of his mettle.

But Regina was not at all entranced with Tristam Barclay, and she turned a disapproving back on him to cross to the other side of the room. From there she witnessed the arrival of the Debenhams.

Lord Grantham was disturbingly handsome in formal dinner clothes, and he greeted his host and hostess with a distinguished bow. Miss Debenham extended a limp hand and allowed Mrs. Dawlish to take it fleetingly. The earl, when he spied Regina, crossed casually to her side and spoke too softly for anyone to overhear. "Well, my sweet dissident, I see your stratagems have failed."

Annoyed at his unwarranted familiarity, Regina's response was formal. "Good evening, my lord. And to what stratagems do you refer?"

"What? You have more than one plot in hand? Never mind, you may still foster a quarrel between the two lovers," Lord Grantham said thoughtfully. "Yes, that might do very well."

The fact that Regina had considered that very possibility did nothing to allay her indignation that the earl would assume that she was out to make mischief. In freezing tones she replied,

"I believe that the marriage will take place August third, and since the principals are satisfied with the arrangement, neither you nor I need concern ourselves further than to think on a gift."

"You are perfectly right, dear girl, and I only hope you mean it. By the way, you are looking very fetching tonight. And the rose in your hair . . . charming."

Regina's hand rose instinctively to touch her coiffure. Celia had insisted on fussing with it tonight, claiming such lovely hair should not be hidden away. Regina had finally consented unwillingly to the addition of a yellow rosebud. "Do not attempt flattery, my lord. I am not susceptible. At my age I know how to rate such pleasantries for the false coin they are. And try to cure yourself of the unfortunate habit of referring to me by these puerile misnomers. The name is Cressley."

Regina swept away from his mocking glance and greeted Miss Margaret more effusively than she intended. She was almost as displeased with her second conversation as with her first. Lord Grantham's persiflage was becoming most vexing, and he showed a deplorable lack of delicacy in insisting that their former relationship gave him the privilege of addressing her in those free and easy terms. He needed to be taught a lesson, and she resolved to leave him strictly alone for the rest of the evening.

At the dinner table Regina found herself seated between Tom and Mr. Barclay while the earl was at Mrs. Dawlish's right hand. Regina was far enough away that her studied avoidance of his eye could seem the merest coincidence.

Mr. Barclay had kept their end of the table in a ripple of laughter for most of the evening. Tom leaned over to Regina. "Isn't he a great gun? The funniest fellow in the world. Monday we're going up to London and see *The Importance of Being Earnest* again. We saw it when it first opened, but, as Tristam says, it repays close examination."

Across the table the vicar smiled benignly. "A play, is it? I think I've heard of it. Any play by that title must be worthy of attention."

"I don't believe it is what you think, Uncle," Regina said cautiously.

Margaret was shocked. "It was written by That Man, and is undoubtedly depraved in its morals."

"Oh, no, Miss Debenham. Tom told me all about it, and it is the most delightful comedy!" Celia protested.

"You are much too young to be a judge of such things," was the lady's verdict.

"What man?" the vicar asked innocently.

After a short but uncomfortable pause, Tristam Barclay spoke urbanely. "Oscar Wilde, sir. He has but recently been remanded to Holloway Prison."

"Why, what has he done?" Celia asked in equal innocence.

"Offended someone very powerful. The Marquess of Queensberry, I believe," Mr. Barclay said with an ironic twist to his lips.

"But . . ." Celia attempted to pursue the

subject, but a warning look from Tom made her subside.

"Really, we should change the subject," quavered Mrs. Dawlish, her naturally nervous disposition causing her to rattle her fork noisily against her spoon. She gave her husband an imploring glance, but as the squire never read anything other than the cricket scores in *The Times*, he had no idea what was making everyone so damned uncomfortable, except that it had to do with that bounder Barclay.

Tristam Barclay spoke up again, this time in sheer deviltry. "Mr. Wilde is a great genius, and future generations will condemn his persecution as an act of barbarism."

Evidently the earl was of the same opinion. He had been staring thoughtfully at Barclay and now came forth in approbation for what was clearly a minority view. "I agree, sir, that the world has been unduly harsh with Wilde. Yet he did bring their wrath down on his own head with that slander suit."

Barclay was rather surprised that his support should come from such an unlikely source. Then he remembered that Grantham was known to be somewhat of a liberal. His sister, obviously, didn't share his view.

Margaret had been growing steadily more indignant that the dinner conversation should have sunk to such depths. "That Man merits no further discussion at this table. His name is repugnant to anyone in decent society." A dark glance at Barclay adjoined this statement. "I suggest," she went on as if it were a royal decree, "that the squire propose a toast for the occasion." She raised her goblet as the ill-prepared squire got hurriedly to his feet.

"Yes, yes." He splashed some wine into his empty glass. "Dear friends, I would like to propose a toast to Celia and Tom." Then, realizing that this part had already been announced, he finished with a flourish, "May they live long and happily." Quite satisfied that he had managed his part admirably, the squire glanced at Miss Margaret for approval. She nodded and everyone rose obediently to salute the blushing young couple.

Tristam Barclay raised his glass also, but there was a sardonic smile visible under his impressive moustache. "To marriage," he added, "an institution on which all women agree, and all men disagree."

Everyone looked at him with varying expressions of uncertainty. Only the earl and Regina understood Barclay's jest, and their eyes met in instant recognition. The jibe was undoubtedly a quote from Wilde. Regina repressed a smile and looked away quickly as Tom drank off his glass with a laugh. The rest took their cue from him and drank as well.

"It's quite extraordinary, isn't it, what a large percentage of those present have managed to avoid the blessings of matrimony," Tristam said blandly. "I wonder if Celia and Tom should do as we say or do as we do?"

Mrs. Dawlish made little squeaks of protest, but the vicar was reproving. "Marriage is a sacrament, young man."

"My apologies, Mr. Cressley. I meant no offense. Nevertheless your example is not particularly encouraging. You have never remarried, not even to give your daughter the mother she might be supposed to have needed."

"I could never find anyone to take the place of my own Elizabeth Ann," the vicar said gently, looking at his daughter with affection. "No doubt it was self-indulgent of me to prefer my memories." He sighed.

"Tom had better look at all these sad old bachelors and bless his luck. I think so highly of the state of matrimony that I would emulate these youngsters in a minute, if the right woman would give me a word of encouragement." Lord Grantham spoke with such a fine mixture of seriousness and jovial good humor that a spontaneous smile went around the table, though his sister appeared taken aback, while Regina became unaccountably engrossed in the examination of her dessert fork.

"Ah, the right woman! That is the rub!" Mr. Barclay said, leaning back in his chair. "To tell the truth, I am far too cowardly to dare to approach the right woman. But then, the wrong ones are so infinitely more appealing!"

"And how do you divide us, sir, into right and wrong?" Regina asked with asperity.

"Why, quite simply. The right ones are invariably dull and plain, while the wrong ones may be equally dull, but one is kept from the knowledge of it by the lure of forbidden fruit."

The earl laughed. "It seems an excellent system to insure your continued independence."

"And a very unkind view of my sex," Celia said indignantly.

Her father intervened. "Remember, Proverbs has it, 'Who so findeth a wife findeth a good thing and obtaineth favor of the Lord.'"

Barclay smiled cynically. "But Ecclesiastes tells us, 'And I find more bitter than death the woman, whose heart is snares and nets.'"

Regina was not amused. "Oh, we know who can quote scripture!" she said scornfully.

"I can only claim to be His disciple," Barclay said in mock humility.

Mrs. Dawlish did not understand what her son's friend had said, and gave a doubtful smile, but Miss Margaret frowned at him ferociously. She was quite sure she understood him to have been exceedingly naughty. "You are talking a great deal of bad sense, young man. I do not approve." She turned to the squire and spoke in tones loud enough to carry the entire length of the table. "Who is that fellow who claims to be the Devil's disciple? It is not respectable."

There was an eager hush of anticipation as everyone waited for Barclay's rejoinder, but Tom forestalled his friend by jumping quickly to his defense. "That's unfair, Miss Debenham. Tristam is quite respectable. He is a poet."

"A poet, is he? I never heard of him," she replied crushingly.

Mrs. Dawlish rose trembling from her chair. Ignoring the obvious fact that dessert was yet to be served, she invited the ladies to join her in the drawing room and leave the gentlemen to their cigars.

Regina rather regretted the move, as the evening became quite ordinary after that.

CHAPTER FIVE

Grantly's annual church fête was second in popularity only to Guy Fawkes Day, and when Saturday dawned bright and clear, there was much rejoicing among the inhabitants. By nine o'clock several booths, two large striped tents, and a bunting-draped stage were set up on the spacious lawns of the castle. The allure of this affair rested in good part on the paucity of entertainment ordinarily available. But there was also much to be said for the pleasure of eating seed buns and ice cream in the open air. The main attraction, however, was the castle itself. The church fête was the one time each year that its gardens, maze, and tinkling fountains were open to the public. It was an invitation to frolic on the grass and feed the bad-tempered swans that floated arrogantly on the waters of the pretty little lake. Even though the castle had recently changed hands, losing in the process some of its ancient distinction, Grantly was glad enough to come out in force to see what changes the new owners had effected.

The old duke had been a veritable recluse, so he was not exactly missed. Nevertheless the change was felt by everyone to be a bit of a comedown. Hermit though he was, the gentleman had always come through handsomely for the annual fête, and Grantly was going to be quick to note and criticize any diminution in quality or quantity this year. Fortunately the Thwaits had kept on most of the old staff, and so things were much as usual, or so it seemed to the early arrivals as they streamed through the scrolled iron gates set hospitably wide for the day.

The Thwaits had purchased the rather dilapidated castle, its furnishings, and the surrounding acres shortly before the duke's demise. Jeremy Thwait, who was "something in the city," and his wife and son had moved from a large, comfortable house in Suburbiton to the fifteenth-century castle, but not without some difficulty. Mrs. Thwait hoped that today would be the turning point, and they'd now find the surrounding gentry in a more forgiving spirit. After all, she was doing her best to live up to local tradition.

Actually the Thwaits would have been a perfectly acceptable addition to the neighborhood if they had chosen a more modest dwelling place. It was their determination to live in the castle that the locals found unbearably pushing. Even Mrs. Clarke, who kept the sweet shop, was up in arms. "Flaunting their nasty money at us, and her no lady, neither," was how the estimable Mrs. Clarke put it to her best friend, the postmistress.

Mrs. Thwait was aware of a certain coldness in the village, which she attempted to wear down with repeated references to the "Dear Duke." Needless to say, it did her little good. But having purchased a fully authentic Elizabethan four-poster in which to lay her bourgeois head, Mrs. Thwait felt she was entitled to lay claim to a friendship that never existed.

The vicar seemed oblivious to the undercurrents that seethed in his parish. If he was aware of Mrs. Thwait's social ambitions or the maneuverings designed to thwart them (the Thwart Thwait Movement, as Celia had dubbed it laughingly to Regina), he gave no sign. Gratefully he had accepted the offer to use the castle grounds again this year, and even more gratefully, taken the large donation from Mr. Thwait. Meanwhile Celia was more or less successful in seeing that Stephen Thwait was included in the social life of the village, as they were both of an age. Tom wasn't overly fond of Stephen, but he enjoyed the many amenities available at the castle enough to disregard his mild dislike.

The Cressleys came early, but already a fair number of people were crowding around the lemonade booth and looking over the jumble tables. Regina was introduced to Mrs. Thwait immediately.

"Charmed, I'm sure," said Mrs. Thwait in paralyzingly refined vowels. She proceeded to overwhelm Miss Cressley with a catalogue of all that the "Dear Duke" had left to them, neglecting to mention that a bill was included in the "inheritance." "You must see the picture gallery," she effused. "So many of the family portraits have a startling likeness to me."

"Really? How interesting," Regina replied politely, wondering if it was Mrs. Thwait's rather close-set eyes or her receding chin that she shared with the duke's forebears.

"Dear Vicar, you will say a few words this afternoon? We need a bit of uplift to fill out the day. Say about two o'clock? The crowd should be nice and thick then," Mrs. Thwait pleaded.

"Well, I could . . ." Mr. Cressley was doubtful. "But we've never done it before. Are you sure they'll listen?"

"Of course! You are so eloquent! And if we remind them of why they are here, not just to enjoy themselves, but to raise money for the church, I'm sure they will be generous!"

"If you think it will help, I have no objection," the vicar sighed. "Goodness knows, it will take a fortune to repair the roof. Dry rot," he added in explanation to Regina before wandering off to look at the pitch-penny stand, where the children were gathered.

Mrs. Thwait gazed around with justifiable pride. Having a speaker was an innovation, she explained. "It adds a certain tone, don't you agree? I'm surprised the Dear Duke didn't think of it himself."

"The duke rarely came out of his room these last ten years," Celia reminded her.

"What a shame! Just think how pleased the villagers would have been to hear directly from such a great nobleman."

Knowing how much the great nobleman had owed the local tradesmen, Celia could imagine their heartfelt joy if he had made it possible for them to present their bills in person. But Mrs. Thwait's notions of the nobility transcended mere monetary obligations. She had almost managed to forget just how parsimonious the Dear Duke had been over the sale of his home. It was Mr. Thwait who finally argued him into a more reasonable asking price. Even then the local tradesmen had to wait until the estate was settled before they could claim recompense.

Mrs. Thwait now expressed another inspiring idea. "I might venture to say a few words myself. On behalf of the Dear Duke, you understand."

Regina agreed that there was nothing like a good speech at the end of a long day and easily convinced her hostess that the crowds would definitely be disappointed if the chatelaine of the castle did not make a contribution along that line herself.

While Mrs. Thwait bustled back indoors to prepare her "few words of welcome," the two girls strolled away to take their turn behind the counter of the stitchery booth.

Celia pinched her cousin's arm. "Regina, how could you? Father will ramble on for an hour at least. If we have to listen to her as well, we'll be bored to death before we can escape."

"You mean you aren't fascinated? I long to hear how the Dear Duke can rest easily in his grave, with the family traditions being carried on so nobly in his name."

"You monster! You mean you will leave me to

sit under father's eye while you eat cake in the refreshment tent."

On the other side of the grounds Tristam Barclay mopped his brow with a snowy handkerchief.
"Devilish boring here, Tom. Don't see why we
came. Since I've done my duty and bought a
perfectly hideous vase for the enormous sum of
sixpence, I suggest we find more congenial
surroundings. I've had enough of that cow, Mrs.
Thwait, to last me an eon or so. The lemonade she
spilled on my jacket will never come out. Lemonade! No one over the age of six should be asked to
consume such swill."

"Come on, Tristam, it doesn't even show."

"But my dear boy, I know it's there. I must
change."

"I promised to have lunch with Celia," Tom
said doubtfully.

"In that ghastly tent? My boy, you are a hero!
Well then, I'll toddle off. There's a train to London at twelve forty I should just be able to
catch."

"You're going up to town?"

"Yes, I'm afraid too much quiet and fresh air
are deleterious to my health," Tristam explained
seriously.

Tom laughed. "Oh, Tristam! Wait, I'll go with
you. I'll just tell Celia."

The stitchery booth had several customers when
Tom made his hurried apologies to his fiancée.
With Regina, Stephen Thwait, and two elderly
ladies for an audience, Celia could only paste a

pleasant smile on her lips and say good-bye. Tom, never the most perceptive of fellows, was just vaguely aware that he was disappointing her. "You're a brick!" he exclaimed. "Tristam and I will be back Tuesday. Shall I bring you something from London?"

Celia shook her head, and Tom disappeared with a wave of his hand. She turned a bright, hard smile on Stephen. "Now what do you fancy? A lovely crocheted antimacassar? Or these baby booties?"

"I'll buy anything you say I should. All of it, in fact, if you'll come take a walk with me now." Stephen pulled a five-pound note out of his pocket and grinned mischievously.

Before Celia could decline, Regina accepted the money. "Thank you, Mr. Thwait. That's very generous. Go on, Celia. You're excused. I'll stay here until Mrs. Clarke can take over."

"Are you sure you can manage?" Celia asked gratefully.

"I promise to make change accurately and not decamp with the profits. Now go along with you and have a nice time." Regina watched the two walk away with relief. There is nothing like the attention of another admirer to heal the wounds that lovers inflict.

Mr. Thwait was also present that morning. A blunt-faced man, large and outwardly affable, he stalked through the grounds with his hands clasped behind his thick back, surveying the animated view before him. He was well aware that many of the people now enjoying his hospitality would have cut him dead if they had met him on the street the week before. They came today out of curiosity and because the long-standing tradition of the fête gave them an excuse to indulge it. Jeremy Thwait cared not a penny for their good-will for himself, but he did want it for the sake of his wife. She had her heart set on making a place for herself in country society. Knowing the power of his immense wealth, it amused him to think he could buy and sell any of these local gentry for all their long-nosed disdain.

Stephen would step up a notch in the world, for sure. There wasn't a blue blood in England who wouldn't jump at the chance to marry his son, he'd wager. But for Stephen, he'd as soon see him choose a nice girl from the same class as his own, a sensible girl with a bit of cash.

Mr. Thwait noticed that his son's gallantries were focused on Miss Celia Cressley, a waste of time since everyone knew that vicars are as poor as their own church mice. But when his wife had told him of meeting the vicar's niece, a Regina Cressley from Manchester, he whistled softly. He had spent so little time in the village it had quite escaped his notice that the unworldly vicar and his pretty daughter were related to the Miss Cressley of Cressley Limited. That was another kettle of fish altogether.

Jeremy Thwait had only recently been approached by someone from that firm. It was supposed to be a dark secret, of course, though the deal was almost closed. Colonel Pucey had insisted on keeping a low profile, and while Jeremy Thwait knew he was on to a good thing, making deals behind closed doors was not his meat. He was an open and aboveboard kind of man, he claimed, besides wanting to show the world how clever he was. Still, Pucey had insisted that Miss Cressley be kept in ignorance of his plans, or she might attempt to forestall his takeover. So, though it was against his nature, Jeremy Thwait made no overture to Regina, but stood watching her from a distance.

Regina had seen him off and on all morning. At first she wondered who was the stocky middle-aged man who kept staring at her. Whenever he caught her eye, he whirled around and scuttled off into the crowd. It was Celia who told her he was Jeremy Thwait.

"I wonder what he's up to?" Regina mused aloud, having second thoughts about the advisability of arranging a meeting with the man. If he was chary of encountering her, it must mean there was something afoot. Best to play along and see what developed.

Celia, though, saw nothing alarming in Thwait's manner. "I've met him several times, and he is quite ordinary. It could be that he is overwhelmed by your charms but is too shy to come and meet you."

Since the girl knew nothing about the situation, her teasing could be excused as youthful spirits, but when Regina again looked to the spot where

Thwait had been standing, he was gone. It was most provoking, almost as much as John's inexplicable behavior. Why hadn't he answered her cablegram?

At long last Mrs. Clarke arrived to take her turn at the booth, and Regina was free to wander through the crowds and search for Celia and Stephen. Peeking into the empty conservatory, she was lured by the intoxicating scent of tropical flowers and stepped inside. The warmth and humidity almost sent her rushing out again until, from the far corner, a giggle and a loud, smacking kiss startled her into immobility. Cautiously looking through the leaves of a large palm tree, Regina was witness to a most interesting tableau.

"Oh, Squire, really, do stop. I must get back to work."

"Naughty puss. Give us another kiss first."

The voice was husky with passion but undoubtedly one Regina had heard before. She turned silently and fled out the door. So Squire Dawlish liked a bit of slap and tickle, did he? And he wasn't too fussy with whom. *There's a good example of a happily married man for you,* Regina thought cynically. More determined than ever to find Celia and head home, she paused by the refreshment tent, but a quick glance inside showed Celia was not there either.

"Not hungry after all?"

Regina looked up into a pair of familiar gray eyes, and Lord Grantham took her arm. "Has your family deserted you, Miss Cressley? Never

86

mind. The rose garden is lovely this time of year."

She allowed him to lead her away from the crowd and settle her on a secluded bench that was set picturesquely among the blooming rose-bushes. Regina sighed blissfully. "This is marvelous," she said. "I've been on my feet for ages . . . selling doilies, no less."

"That seems rather like using a cannon to kill flies: a waste of firepower."

"Is that a compliment? I don't care for the metaphor. But where is your sister? I haven't seen her today."

"Maggie pleaded a headache, but in truth, she does not like to encourage social climbers. Besides, the Thwaits are in trade, and that alone calls for social ostracism." His tone held a slight mockery for Margaret's snobbishness, although he said nothing to apologize for it.

"Then I'm surprised she tolerates me."

"Oh, you haven't tried to oust her as the arbiter of fashion in the neighborhood."

"You mean Mrs. Thwait has? How very brave of her!" Regina laughed.

"The castle outshines Grantly Priory, I'm afraid, but as the old duke never entertained, Margaret had it all her own way for donkey's years. She's outraged that the Thwaits, who are nobody, of course, besides being enormously rich, should try to challenge her position. You are quite right to laugh; it is absurd."

Regina looked at him silently. His sister's foibles were no doubt amusing, but was it well done of him to discuss them with a comparative stranger? But then, he insisted on treating her as if she were not a mere acquaintance, rather like . . . Regina groped for the word, but it eluded her.

The earl continued lightly. "And how goes the young Miss Cressley's romance? Have the lovers quarreled yet?"

"It's not a joke, Alistair," she sighed, not realizing that by dropping his title, she had acknowledged the intimacy of their relationship.

The earl, in contrast, was very well aware of her unguarded admission, and he stepped lightly. "You really are cast down, Regina. Tell me. Perhaps I can help."

His voice was sympathetic, and for once she could detect no mockery in his tone, but she shook her head. How could she discuss Tom's appalling behavior? Celia would appear in the pathetic role of the wronged woman. It was too demeaning. Deflecting the conversation from Tom and Celia, she said, "I have a worry or two, but I'm afraid it is just dull business."

Regina expected that this would close the subject. In her experience, no one was interested in such matters. Her mother claimed that it bored her to death. So when Regina talked business, it was always to sell her ideas or to convince the doubtful. There had never been anyone to simply listen and sympathize.

"I heard that someone is selling off a big block

of your company's stock, and that Thwait wants to buy."

Regina turned. "You heard?"

"There are always rumors on the Exchange. But I suppose you want those shares yourself. Don't look so surprised. I speculate on the market, and I've kept an eye on Cressley Limited over the years. A sentimental interest, you might say."

Regina had no intention of allowing that bit of flattery to weigh with her, yet her answer indicated a softening of her attitude. "Yes, I do plan to buy those shares, although I am a little concerned just now. I haven't heard from John Lassiter in weeks, and Jeremy Thwait has been melting away whenever I've come within eyesight of him."

"Sounds as if Thwait's beaten you to it."

"That's impossible. John wouldn't do anything so underhanded."

"Then why hasn't he sold to you already?"

"It is only a matter of time," Regina tossed off, though she wondered the same thing herself. It was unlike John to keep her dangling. He was only leading on Colonel Pucey, she was sure. That would be like John's puckish sense of humor. But did he realize he was also subjecting Regina to the same treatment? If Dottie's unflattering appraisal of the feckless John Lassiter was true, he was only after the highest bid, and even friendship wouldn't stand in his way. Regina wasn't quite ready to believe the worst of him yet, but bother the man for playing jokes without letting her in on them.

The earl politely accepted Regina's excuse, though his expression indicated a certain skepticism. "Then let's change the subject. You are in looks today, Ginny. Life away from your desk seems to agree with you."

"The stupidest things impress you, Alistair. It's just a change in hairstyle, and I only did it to make Celia happy. Personally I think I look ridiculous. That's probably the reason you spirited me off to the rose garden . . . so you wouldn't be seen talking to me."

"It wasn't talking I had in mind."

"Then you are doomed to disappointment. Why not take a lesson from the squire? He has quite a practiced way with the ladies."

The earl looked at her sharply. "Did he try something with you?"

"Don't be silly. Of course not. You sound almost indignant. But then, harassing me is solely your privilege. No, I saw the squire in the conservatory, plying his wiles on a servant. Poor Mrs. Dawlish. How does she put up with it?"

"They seem quite happy."

"What you mean is that she pretends not to know what's going on because she has no choice. It's wretchedly unfair. I pity Celia."

"You are not accusing Tom of being a womanizer, are you? I assure you, he is quite devoted to Celia."

"But not so devoted to her as he is to Mr. Barclay. And women are not that man's weakness, I'm afraid. I only hope Tom is not of the same disposition."

"That's a libelous accusation," he said after a moment.

"Why do you think the squire is so eager for Tom to marry my penniless cousin? Surely you know Barclay's reputation."

"Because of his emulation of Wilde? You're as bad as the other old biddies."

"I don't care what his preferences are, but what about Tom? Is it fair to marry him off to an innocent like Celia in the hope that her influence will counteract Barclay's?"

"You could be wrong about Tom."

"If there weren't some truth to it, why is his father in such a panic? It makes me furious that no one but me seems concerned about Celia's happiness."

"The role of judge and executioner doesn't suit you, Regina."

"You forget, I'm not a child, Alistair. Nor am I a prude. These oddities don't repel me. But when they affect someone I love, then it is another matter. Closing our eyes to the existence of danger doesn't make it go away. You pretend it doesn't exist. The squire, at least, battles for his side as I do for mine."

"Battles? What an odd choice of words. Or is it? You do love a fight, don't you, Regina? In fact, you could have given pointers to Napoleon."

91

"I respect anyone who fights for what he wants. Nothing worth having comes easily."

"And I gave up too tamely twelve years ago. Did you want me to fight back, Regina love? Convince you against your will that you should marry me?"

"Must you always drag in the personal? I was just making a generalization."

"I've learned that generalizations like that are based on the personal. Did I insult you by accepting your refusal too easily?"

"On the contrary. I was pleased that you showed such perception."

"I wonder. Doesn't it get lonely with just a bank account for company at night?"

"You are being vulgar, Lord Grantham." Regina turned away in disapproval.

"So you've become a prig. How disappointing. I had hoped that with age you might have loosened up a bit. Since we are both older and presumably wiser now, our relationship should not be so constricted. Come now, Regina, you must admit there is something between us still. Or why are you sitting here listening to me instead of manipulating tea cozies?"

Regina hid a smile. She was not displeased at the thought that he was still interested in her, but she wasn't so sure she wanted to return the compliment. Alistair had a potent charm, and he was expending a great deal of it to win her over. But Regina was not foolish enough to be persuaded that he meant much by it. It was only a game to him, recapturing the affections of the girl he had once lost. The earl didn't want her as such, only her admission that she still found him attractive, not an impossible thing to concede. If a man has done nothing worse than propose marriage, he can surely keep the woman's friendship.

"I'm not adverse to a kindly disposition between us, my lord."

"Is that the best you can do?"

"What more do you want?"

"Something, shall we say, a bit more spirited."

Regina said nothing to this, finding the implication disquieting.

But Lord Grantham was quick to take advantage of her silence. He slipped one arm around her shoulders and tilted her face up to his. "Why not give it a try, Regina? You might even find you like it."

His mouth was about to descend on hers when she jumped up in sudden panic. "None of that, if you please."

"But, dear girl, how can you play the game if you don't abide by the rules? An experimental kiss or two is not capitulation. You can still call halt whenever you choose."

"I should have known your intentions were dishonorable," Regina accused. "How stupid of me. A man can never be satisfied with friendship."

"That depends on the intimacy of the friendship," he joked. "A little less reserve might yield some surprises for you." He took her unresisting hand and stroked it softly.

"Why don't you go pick on someone your own size," Regina said gruffly, snatching her abused hand away.

"You are my perfect size."

"On the off-chance that you haven't been listening, I am declining your offer of an . . . an . . ."

"An affair?" he finished for her. "My, you do go from point A to C without considering B. Never mind. If it's an affair you want, an affair you'll get."

Regina spun around and headed down the walk, the echo of his laughter behind her. When he made no effort to catch up, she slowed her pace and reached the crowded lawn with some semblance of calm. She wasted no more time searching for Celia, and walked back to the vicarage alone.

CHAPTER SIX

A false calm settled over the vicarage after the church fête, but Tom's defection weighed heavily on Celia. Regina unwisely exacerbated her discontent by pointing out the obvious.

"The problem is that you are too docile, Celia. You allow Tom to neglect you. It's time you told him that you will not tolerate his putting Barclay before you. If you don't do something now, it will only be worse when you marry!"

Regina was overemphatic, but a second letter from Dottie Hodgekiss had her nerves on edge. It seemed that Thwait had raised his bid on Lassiter's shares, and John, still in Italy, had wired the office of this development.

Regina was finding it hard to believe that John could be so mercenary, but the evidence was piling up against him. The price Thwait was offering was already an inflated figure, and John still made no move to sell. Evidently he was playing Regina against Thwait to get the highest possible price. Of course, Lassiter was not just selling shares in the company, but control of Cressley Limited; and that was another game entirely. The joke had lost its humor for Regina.

She cabled another bid, but it was with an anxious heart that she awaited the reply. In the beginning she had relied on John's loyalty. Now she could no longer believe that such feelings would count with him. It was simply a battle of the pocketbook. Possibly, Thwait might lose interest if it became too expensive, but Regina thought it an unlikely contingency. Money would not weigh with him once he was determined on a course of action.

When Tom returned on Tuesday, the gathered tensions showed themselves in a surprising way. Driving over to the vicarage in his car, Tom found Celia returning from a ride with Stephen Thwait. The two cantered into the yard as Tom waited by his green Daimler.

"Why, Tom, I didn't expect you back so soon," Celia exclaimed as Stephen helped her dismount. "Did you have a nice time?"

Tom glared in surprise at the couple strolling over to him. "Hullo, Celia, Stephen," he said grudgingly.

Stephen smiled coolly at him, then turned to Celia. "I'm off. Frightfully charming afternoon. Let's do it again. Saturday?"

"Oh, Stephen, it was lovely. Yes, Saturday would be fine. 'Bye!"

Swinging himself into the saddle, Stephen took the reins of Celia's piebald and trotted off.

For a moment Tom looked after him, noting his fine seat and easy hand on the horses, but then he grunted, "Bloody show-off."

"Tom!" Celia admonished.

"Sorry, but the fellow is nothing but a vulgar upstart. What was he doing here anyway?"

"Stephen only took me riding."

"Only, my foot. What's this about Saturday? I'll not have him poaching. You shouldn't be seeing anyone but me. We're engaged, remember?"

"Am I supposed to sit at home alone when you run off to London with Tristam Barclay? I don't see you curtailing any of your pleasures for me. At least Stephen is considerate of my feelings," Celia said sharply. She walked into the house, leaving her open-mouthed fiancé standing on the porch.

Tom was astounded. Never before had he seen her like this. What was she angry about? He hadn't done a thing to offend her, he told himself resentfully. Clamping his lips together, he marched after her on a wave of righteous indignation. She had no business seeing Thwait when his back was turned.

"What right has that bounder to take you riding?" he demanded angrily.

"Right?" Celia questioned, tossing her gloves on the table with undue force. "I don't think 'rights' have anything to do with it. Stephen is just a very kind person. He saw I needed cheering up."

"Doesn't he know you are engaged?"

Celia looked at Tom's angry face with cold dislike. "Do you?"

"What kind of question is that? Of course I do. I haven't looked at another girl for ages now."

"Really? Not even in London? Not even at

those gay little theater parties that your friend Barclay gets up?" Celia asked skeptically.

He stared at her as if she had gone mad. "Who's been filling your head with nonsense? There are women in London who are my friends, but it's nothing for you to worry about. They're not important, not like you!" Tom was at a loss how to handle this girl who was looking at him with such chilly disapproval. Where was the adoring light he was accustomed to seeing in her eyes? "Has Thwait said something to you? I'll thrash him within an inch of his life."

"Stephen said nothing about you, Tom. You'd do better to ask yourself what you have done instead."

"It's your cousin then. She never liked me."

Celia had to control an urge to smooth the stubborn curl that had fallen over his forehead. He looked like a confused little boy who was being reprimanded for an unknown crime. Yet that was the point. He wasn't a boy anymore, and that youthful charm had to face up to the responsibility of adulthood. To Tom their engagement was just a carefree prelude to playing house. He had no conception of what marriage really meant. Celia could see this now, and she hardened her heart. If there was any chance for them, Tom had to face the truth. Celia didn't want to mother him forever, kiss away his hurts and coax him out of the sullens. She wanted to do a bit of leaning herself, otherwise she would just be trading a helpless father for a helpless husband. Then, too, there was the matter of Tristam Barclay.

"I promise you, Tom, that no one has said anything. Don't blame Stephen Thwait for showing me some kindness. It's more than you've done. How would you like it if I rushed off at every opportunity? You spend more time with Tristam Barclay than you do with me."

"What's wrong with Tristam? I suppose your cousin Regina has been talking against him. Tristam said she was a spiteful cat. She disliked him the moment she set eyes on him."

"Then she has more sense than you do. And I agree with her. I despise the man." Celia stopped in sudden confusion. She hadn't meant to blurt out her feelings like that, but now that it was said, she felt a certain relief. "I'm sorry, Tom. I know it sounds harsh, but it's the truth. I dislike everything about Barclay: his posturing, his conceit, his spiteful remarks. But most of all, I can't stand the way he leads you around by the nose. Barclay snaps his fingers, and you jump."

For the first time since Celia had come into his life with her quiet adoration, she was criticizing him, and it stung. "That's not true! Tristam is a brilliant, talented man and my best friend. You're just jealous."

"Jealous! Well, perhaps I am. You care more for that . . . that toad than you do for me."

Tom drew himself up with an attempt at dignity. "I would never have believed it of you, Celia. You are trying to dictate to me! A man has a right to his friends. I can't spend every minute with you. Being engaged doesn't mean we are chained to each other."

"Chained together? Is that what you think I want? It's fine for you to go to London for days on end, but I must not go riding with a friend! It seems the chains are for me, at least." Celia's eyes shone with indignation.

"Well, of course. The two things are quite different," Tom said firmly. "You are my girl, aren't you?"

"Oh, Regina was right!" Celia turned away to hide the angry tears that threatened to spill over.

"Regina! Ha! So she has been filling your head with some sort of women's rights nonsense. You tell her to stay out of this. A dried-up old maid, what does she know? Come here and give me a kiss and be my sweet Celia again, and we'll forget the whole thing."

Celia faced him with difficulty. He was smiling at her now, confident that everything was settled. "Don't you see, Tom, it's not Regina; it's you. Marriage shouldn't be chains for anyone. I want you to put me first because you want to, not because you must." Celia pulled off the small, perfect sapphire he had given her less than a week before. "I'm sorry, Tom."

"What! Celia, you don't mean it." Furiously he waved away the proffered ring. "That cousin of yours will be sorry. Put the ring back on, Celia. This minute!"

Celia was regretting her gesture of bravado already, but the peremptory tone of Tom's voice stiffened her resolve. She put the ring down on the table. "It's either Barclay or me. You have to choose."

His eyes demanded she retract her challenge, but when Celia showed she could be just as stubborn, Tom snatched up the ring. "I suppose you think you can do better. Well, I wish you joy with Stephen Thwait!" And he stormed out of the house without a backward glance.

Celia stared after him in shocked dismay. This couldn't be happening. Tom should have been at her feet now, begging her forgiveness and promising to cut Barclay out of his life forever. Instead, her worst fears had been confirmed.

She turned blindly from the solidly closed front door and faced the unpalatable truth: Barclay had somehow won. It was he who now had first claim on Tom's loyalty and affections. Her ultimatum had only given Tom the excuse he needed to make that final choice. A flash of anger strengthened her sense of outrage. That stupid, childish, selfish boy! Regina was right. Tom wasn't worthy of her devotion, and she was well rid of him. If he truly preferred Barclay to her, he was welcome to him. But even that justifiable reasoning did not prevent her from promptly bursting into tears and running up to her room, where she remained for the rest of the day.

The broken engagement was the talk of the village. Celia and Tom had been so devoted, so in love. But Stephen Thwait's attentions had not gone unnoticed, and most people were saying that Celia had jilted Tom for a chance at a wealthier man. Celia merely gave fuel to the gossip by being very gay and spending a great deal of time with Stephen.

When Regina tried to talk to her about it, the girl simply said that they had quarreled and that it was all over. "You were right, Regina. Marriage to Tom would have been a mistake."

Regina looked at the hard expression on Celia's face and worried. "Was it because of what I said, dear?"

"No, not really. You just made me face up to the facts."

And when Regina renewed her offer of a trip to Europe in the fall, her cousin agreed that it sounded nice.

Yet, despite all her original misgivings about the match, Regina could not feel easy about Celia's sudden termination of the engagement. The girl said she was happy, but her serene calm was gone. Instead, there was a shell of bright chatter that kept everyone at a distance. The vicar said little about his daughter's changed plans, but withdrew more and more from family life, turning reproachful eyes on his niece whenever they met.

Regina fully expected Tom to come by those first few days, but he made no attempt to see Celia. His parents were not so proud. Regina was not present at the interview, but she saw the subdued couple as they climbed into their trap and headed back to the Grange. Mrs. Dawlish's eyes were red.

As the days passed, Regina wasn't sure why she didn't jump on the next train to Manchester. Celia was too busy with Stephen Thwait to be much company for her. And with everything ostensibly resolved, time was heavy on her hands. Maybe it was simply a sense of responsibility that kept her in Grantly, as it was her interference that had triggered this dismal situation. Leaving now would seem almost like deserting. Regina was sure that Celia loved Tom as much as ever, and that her feverish absorption with Stephen Thwait was only an attempt to show Tom that she wasn't nursing a broken heart. Tom was playing the same sort of game, for he was still in Grantly, spending all his time with Barclay. Perhaps Regina was just waiting for the inevitable reconciliation to take place so that she could return to Manchester with a clear conscience. But that was only part of her hesitation to leave.

In a pensive mood Regina took out Celia's bicycle one afternoon. A wooded path stretched between the castle and Grantham Priory, and Regina welcomed the stillness and solitude, letting the soft breeze and whispering leaves soothe her troubled spirits. She was gliding down a gentle decline that curved to the right when a solitary horseman rounded the bend. She braked and pulled over to the grassy verge as Lord Grantham cantered over.

"Good afternoon. The vicar said you'd taken the bicycle out this way." He smiled wickedly.

"Very pretty ankles, Ginny. You should show them more often."

The divided skirt was Celia's and at least two inches shorter on Regina than modesty dictated. But it was convenient for bicycling so Regina took it, though she was not best pleased that Lord Grantham was the one to see her in it. Her memory still burned from their last encounter. "How d'you do," she said neutrally.

He dismounted and led the horse over to where Regina stood beside the bicycle. His riding gear gave him a rather rugged appearance, with jodhpurs that hugged his muscular legs and a thick white sweater that accented the dark contrast of his hair. Suddenly Regina was very aware of him.

"Are congratulations in order?" he asked, barring her passage down the lane.

As usual, Regina had no difficulty in understanding the earl's teasing attempts to disconcert her. "Stop it, Alistair. I had nothing to do with the broken engagement. It was all Celia's idea, and I'm not at all happy about it."

"So you've decided that the remedy is worse than the disease."

"Remedy?"

"Stephen Thwait."

He was altogether too perceptive, Regina thought with a prick of discomfort. "I cannot like him," she allowed, "but that is Celia's decision."

"So you've had enough of interfering in your cousin's love life. Now Celia can make her own mistakes without your help. That is generous of you, Regina."

Her temper flared at this all too accurate appraisal. "Must you be facetious? Perhaps my advice carried more weight with her than I thought. But I didn't plant the seed, Alistair. It was already there. Why do you think I came to Grantly? It was to find out why Celia herself had reservations about the betrothal."

"I see. You didn't have a thing to do with it. There's a lovely pond over there in the woods. Let's go look at it."

"I haven't time," she prevaricated. "Celia is expecting me back at any minute."

"She's out for the day with Stephen; I passed them on the road. Come, come, Regina. I promise to protect you from any dangers."

"And who will protect me from you?" she asked pointedly. Nevertheless she allowed him to tie his horse to a low branch and prop the bicycle against another tree trunk. Pushing an opening in the hedge with his booted foot, he lifted Regina easily and set her down on the other side. A two-minute walk found them in an open glade where a chuckling brook widened into a small pond. A break in the trees let the sun shine warmly on a sweet-smelling, grassy bank.

The earl pulled Regina down onto the warm grass, then stretched himself full length beside her with a grunt of lazy satisfaction. "I knew you'd like it," he commented at her silence, letting his long legs dangle precariously close to the water's edge.

Regina sat stiffly beside him, very much on guard. Why had she let him talk her into coming to this isolated, if pretty, spot?

"You look like a young girl with your hair down your back. No, don't hide it away in that wretched scarf. All you need is a satchel of books on your arm, and you could pass for a schoolroom lass." He took a length of silky hair and wound it around his fingers. "Did you know that your ears look deliciously edible?"

Regina shied at the intimacy of his words and looked away from the dangerous gleam in his eye. "Shouldn't you be working at whatever important landowners do in the country?"

"I'm taking some well deserved time off for good behavior. I've been a paragon of virtue since the fête."

"I was wondering how long it would be before you dragged up that episode. You behaved disgracefully."

He smiled. "So that's what I was doing? I could have sworn I was making love to you."

"Improper suggestions, you mean."

"Then I'm surprised you came along with me now."

Since Regina couldn't answer that satisfactorily to herself, she invented an excuse before he could draw his own perverse conclusions. "I needed to get away for a while and your offer of a pond and a quiet corner seemed just the medicine."

"So Thwait has bought the shares. I'm sorry, Regina."

"No, certainly not! What gave you that idea? I'm waiting to hear from John, that's all."

"Ah, well. It's not so very important, is it?"

"It's vitally important. It's twelve years of my life. John's stock and mine make a majority. He voted with me on most issues and when he didn't, I lost. I'm managing director of the company to-day because of him. But once Thwait gets that stock, how long do you think I will last? By two minutes into the next board meeting, Colonel Pucey will be in my place."

"Ah, yes. The redoubtable colonel."

"So you've heard of him too. The miserable beast. Ever since I took control of the company, he's been trying to topple me. But I won't let it happen. I didn't get where I am by giving up when the going got difficult."

"Brave words, my dear. But what if you lose?"

Regina shrugged off that possibility. "I won't lose. Once those shares are in my control, I'll never be in danger like this again."

"You are a remarkable woman, Regina. A fighter to the end."

Before, Regina had tolerated this criticism from him, but now she felt it was important to repudiate it. "You wouldn't think there was anything the least remarkable about me if I were a man. Most women could do what I've done, given the same chance."

"I doubt that. You made your opportunity; no

one gave it to you. Most women would be terrified at such a prospect, and few would have the brains to carry it through. Few men would either, for that matter. But the point is, you are a woman. If you were Walter Cressley's son, your succession would have been inevitable. He'd have trained you to take over for him . . . and incidentally, left you controlling interest in the company. No one would have disputed your right to run the business then; it would have been expected. You, in turn, did the unexpected. That's quite an accomplishment for a woman."

"We keep coming back to that, don't we? I'm not a person, I'm a woman."

"Would you have me deny the evidence of my eyes? There are only two kinds, you know. And my sort wears pants and shaves every morning."

"Don't be flippant, Alistair. I simply want to be valued at my real worth, not dismissed as a freak."

"Ginny, be realistic for once in your life. Men like Thwait don't care that you've put your heart and soul into your work. To them your company is just another acquisition. At the end of a day spent juggling profit and loss, they have families to come home to. What do you have? A cold, empty house with no one to care if you're happy or not. If he destroys all your fine dreams, what remains for you?"

"Don't waste your worry on me, Alistair. I know how to take care of myself."

"In business perhaps, but when it comes to your

personal life, all your brilliant acumen flies out the window. You are not only illogical, but more vulnerable than you'd like to admit."

"What do you mean?"

Pulling her down beside him on the soft ground, his mouth found hers with a tender insistence that quickly dispelled Regina's brief flicker of panic. She closed her eyes and returned the kiss, enjoying the gentle mastery that he had over her.

As he pressed her against the hard length of his body, the masculine scent of him teased her senses. It all felt exactly right, even as one corner of her mind clamored that she must stop this foolishness. It was Alistair, now as always, who alone could kindle an ardor that stripped away her careful defenses. Regina made no move to stop him as his mouth trailed a line of kisses from her eyes to the throbbing pulse in her throat. Instead, she drew him closer, feeling all the while like an aging Circe, unsure of her powers, worrying about who might see her lying there in Lord Grantham's arms, and wondering if he was enjoying it as much as she was.

In the end, she did give him what he wanted: a physical admission that she was not indifferent to him. The confession was not as difficult as she feared.

Alistair drew his lips from hers slowly. "This is what I mean," he whispered.

Lying on the grass, her arms still around him, Regina wanted to respond to the passion in his eyes, but she dared not. "It doesn't change anything," she murmured. "A moment's weakness, that's all."

He kissed her eyelids softly. "It changes everything."

For a perilous moment Regina almost succumbed. A bird was singing in the wood, the sunlight was warm on her face, and part of her wanted very much to press Alistair's dark head to her breast and love him. Then she came to her senses. Sitting up abruptly, she pushed him away and said briskly, "That's enough of that."

"I disagree."

"Of course you do." Regina's tone was cordial as she stood up and began brushing off her skirt. "This is all very flattering, my lord, and at my age too." She was smiling to herself, and Alistair thought it quite the most seductive thing he'd ever seen. "But I'm afraid I'm just too old to start something I would be sure to regret."

"You wouldn't regret a thing."

Regina looked down at the earl reclining lazily on the grass, and the sparkle in her eyes sent a very clear message. "Rash words, my lord," she said with a decided challenge in her voice.

The earl only smiled, then stood up with slow grace and inspected her critically. He fastened the top button of her blouse, which Regina had somehow overlooked, and pulled a tuft of grass from her hair. "You'd better brush it. It looks rather tousled."

"Is it very noticeable?" she asked. "I'm afraid I haven't a comb wih me."

"Here, I'll smooth it a bit." She kept a discreet silence as he brushed at her hair and tied it back with the scarf. "It looks better now. A little wind-blown, but that is understandable as you've been out bicycling."

Their walk back to the lane was surprisingly comfortable, as if what they shared was of the most commonplace. At the tree where the earl's horse stood waiting, they paused, looking into each other's eyes.

"It was a memorable battle, Regina. Until the next one."

She mounted her bicycle and pedaled away, leaving Lord Grantham in the tree-shadowed lane. The man was clearly an unprincipled lecher, she decided. A battle indeed. She hummed all the way home.

CHAPTER SEVEN

Miss Margaret Debenham was far from being a stupid woman, though she was ordinarily insensitive to people's moods and feelings. So it wasn't surprising, even if it did take a while to penetrate, that she finally noticed a change in her brother. He was not his usual unflappable self, but veered between elation and uncharacteristic absentmindedness. Margaret had begun to pay attention the night of the engagement party at the Grange, when Alistair expressed an envy of the married state. Perhaps most of those present dismissed his speech as mere politeness, designed to smooth over a moment's awkwardness, but his sister saw the meaningful look he bestowed upon Miss Cressley at the time, and it worried her. After all, he was approaching that age when men are prone to make sudden and disastrous changes in their lives.

At forty many a man looks at his life and shudders with distaste. A few abandon career and family and take off for tropical islands; others find in themselves an unexpected passion for some wildly unsuitable female. Margaret feared that Alistair's aberration was to be unreasonably charmed by Regina Cressley. Reputedly he had actually kissed her in the castle's rose garden.

Even discounting that rumor as an exaggeration, Margaret was troubled enough to ruminate on various strategies as she went about her daily tasks. It might be thought that it was really no concern of hers, as the earl was well past the age of consent. However, since Margaret was quite fond of her younger brother, she was firmly convinced that it was her duty to prevent him from making a fool of himself. Remembering all her past efforts to interest him in a nice girl, Margaret felt a martyr to his stubbornness. What could have attracted him to that dowdy and undoubtedly shrewish hussy anyway? Clearly it was time for a serious diversionary action. If Alistair was now determined to marry, his sister was equally determined that it should be to someone exactly right: a girl from a distinguished family, with a gentle, biddable disposition and a decent amount of money. She needn't be as vulgarly rich as Miss Cressley, of course.

It took a few days of cogitation, but Margaret came up with the perfect candidate. Smiling broadly to herself, she penned a note of invitation that was promptly accepted. Congratulating herself on having made a wise decision, she then prepared for her guests' appearance.

It was Lord Grantham's custom to join his sister in the drawing room immediately after dinner, as he was a moderate drinker and preferred coffee at the end of a meal instead of a glass of port alone at the table. Margaret's objection to this was that he brought his smelly cigar into the drawing room with him, but tonight she was ready to overlook that unfortunate habit. As he was about to take his customary stroll along the terrace to avoid disturbing her, she called for him to come inside and join her by the fire.

He raised his brows in surprise. "Have you developed a fondness for cigar smoke, Maggie?"

"Of course not. A filthy habit. But I do have something to discuss with you." Margaret had never before invited guests to the priory without consulting Alistair first. Not that he was likely to object; in fact, he encouraged her to keep up her social life in the country, knowing that she only left their town residence each summer because he needed her to run the large house for him. But since her purpose was not just a simple house party, she wanted to be sure to avoid any misunderstandings before they arose. "I have asked Bella Farnsworth to come stay for a few weeks."

"I thought you had quarreled with her."

"Quite right. I did. But she is an old friend, and I have decided that bygones should be bygones. The thing is, I need your help with one small problem. Bella is bringing her youngest daughter with her, a charming girl. I'm sure she'll be sought after once the young men see what a beauty we've imported, but until she makes a few friends, I want you to spend time with her. Dimity is an exquisite child, but rather shy of strangers, Bella tells me."

"Aren't I a stranger?" Alistair asked pointedly. "Really, I couldn't undertake to play nanny while you and Bella are busy gossiping. Why don't you ask one of the village girls to come and keep her entertained?"

"You misunderstood me, Allie," Margaret corrected hastily. "She doesn't need a nursemaid. Dimity just had her eighteenth birthday. She will come out next season. Her mother says she is sure to be the prettiest debutante this year."

"Then why bring her to Surrey? There are no eligible bachelors in Grantly unless you count poor Tom Dawlish. And I think the Farnsworths can look higher than a squire's son."

"Now why should you jump to the conclusion that Bella is anxious to marry off her daughter? She just thinks that a fortnight in the country will be a nice change for the girl."

"Doesn't her father have a seat in Hampshire?"

"You are being difficult, Alistair. Bella prefers to visit us just now," Margaret said coolly, a dangerous glint in her eye.

He allowed himself a chuckle at his sister's expense. "Of course she does. I must say, Maggie, your matchmaking is as unsubtle as ever. I thought you had given up after the fiasco with Miss Albermarle. Surely you could not approve of her hiding in my wardrobe."

"You can hardly blame me for that. I was sadly mistaken in her character. Deceived, in fact! She wasn't even the dear viscount's daughter, but the child from his wife's first marriage to some penniless sailor who was, fortunately, lost at sea. But she was my only error. You must admit that my other choices were eminently suitable and almost always charming in their various ways. The thing is, Alistair, you have been abominably hard to please," Margaret concluded in an aggrieved tone.

"Hard to please? Perhaps so, Margaret. But at my age I have no taste for sweet young things. Couldn't you find me a woman of sense? Someone with an idea in her head besides fashion and flirtation?"

Margaret sighed. "Dear boy, you say that is what you want, but speaking bluntly, it is not what you need. You should have married years ago. Since you didn't, you must marry someone young enough to be a mother to your children. Older women are a bad risk. If they are not barren, their health is quite broken by an attempt at child-bearing. And more than that, a young woman will mold herself to suit you. In a year or two she will learn to be the perfect wife. Anyone older, no matter how intelligent or attractive, is inevitably set in her ways. Believe me, at your age you would find it quite difficult to adapt yourself to a strong-minded female with her own peculiarities and tastes."

Alistair eyed the glowing ash on his cigar. Obviously Margaret knew and disapproved of his growing interest in Regina. In her own inimitable way, his sister was pointing out the difficulties without naming names. He smiled mirthlessly. How little she realized that Regina had her own cogent arguments against such a marriage. Why hadn't he married? He'd always meant to, and once even wanted to, quite passionately. That disappointment had kept him from looking around for a longish bit. Later, the girls paraded before him had seemed insipidly young. The years had flown by unnoticed. Fully occupied with a political career, he had allowed the question to become academic, always assuming that he would find the right woman one day.

"Margaret, you are wasting your time," he said pleasantly.

"But you will be kind to Dimity?" she pursued.

"Of course. The soul of hospitality," he promised, smiling sardonically.

"Thank you, dear." Margaret was pleased. She had said what needed saying, and Alistair had listened with attention. He knew now that her motives were quite, quite selfless in all this. And he was too sensible not to realize that she was right, as usual.

The Farnsworths arrived at Grantham Priory the next afternoon and even Margaret was surprised by the breathtaking beauty that stepped down from the carriage that had fetched them from the train station. Just gracefully above middle height, her perfect figure dressed in the latest mode, and with wide-open, long-lashed violet eyes, Dimity was a sight to please all tastes.

Lord Grantham welcomed his guests politely after exchanging an expressive smile with his sister. She had outdone herself this time; she must be really worried. Mrs. Farnsworth, a tall buxom lady with an incipient moustache, presented her daughter with justifiable pride, and a delicate blush spread over the maiden's damask cheeks. "How d'you do, my lord. I'm very pleathed to be here," Dimity lisped sweetly.

Margaret was delighted with her guests. Dimity was everything she'd hoped, even if Bella was more coarse than she remembered. But that was of little account; it was the daughter who mattered. She was certainly lovely enough to make Alistair forget his ridiculous *tendresse* for the spinsterish Miss Cressley.

At dinner that evening Dimity sat quietly while the others carried the conversation. Her eyes remained modestly cast down, and her delicate mouth opened only to nibble a morsel of fish. Yet she drew all eyes by the perfection of her face, with its classical features and rose-petal complexion.

Margaret tried to draw her out. "Do you play the piano, my dear? Perhaps you could give us a little concert after dinner."

The girl looked up, but it was the mother who answered. "Dimity is quite accomplished, but I'm afraid she doesn't play before company. She's very shy, you see." The object of this analysis continued eating placidly as if she were used to such comments.

"Of course," Margaret said faintly, a little daunted. But she continued coaxingly, "And you do ride, Miss Farnsworth? We have some gentle mounts that should suit you."

Mrs. Farnsworth vetoed that idea immediately. "Oh, no. Dimity's only excursions are in a carriage. She must guard her complexion from too much sun. Isn't that right, my precious?"

"Yeth, Mama," came the flutelike voice.

Margaret sat back, temporarily defeated. She was going to have to speak to Bella. How was the girl to captivate Alistair if the mother never allowed her to speak? Margaret glanced anxiously at her brother but was relieved to see him eyeing Miss Farnsworth with interest. He must be charmed by Dimity's modest quiet, so unlike the pert, forward girls one saw so frequently these days.

Alistair had been looking at Miss Farnsworth all evening. She was incredibly lovely, but she reminded him forcefully of nothing so much as a doll. That pure white brow, did it ever wrinkle in thought? Speculatively, he looked at the formidable mama. No lack of character there. It hardly seemed possible that the daughter of such a one could be the complete nullity she appeared. Curiosity prompted him to make a rash offer.

"Perhaps it's time Miss Farnsworth learned to ride," he said, smiling at his guests. "Surely a hat could shield that radiant complexion. I promise that she will come to no harm. Would you like that, Miss Farnsworth?"

Dimity flushed delicately and turned to her mother appealingly. "Could I, Mama? Pleath?"

Mrs. Farnsworth looked mulish, but a meaningful pinch from Margaret tempered her answer.

"Well—" she said unwillingly, "she has no riding habit."

"I have several that I used to wear packed away upstairs," Margaret said smoothly. "With a very little work, they could be altered to fit Dimity. We are much of a height."

Bella had had time to think things over. She'd come to the priory at Margaret's insistence but held little hope that Dimity could interest such a confirmed bachelor as Lord Grantham. Besides, once she made her debut, Dimity would never lack for suitors. Nevertheless, a mild flirtation with a trustworthy older man might be just the thing for the child. It would give her the self-confidence she so sorely needed. And then, of course, if the earl did come up to scratch, what a coup that would be.

Bella assayed a smile. "You will find she is a timid thing, Lord Grantham. You'd best start her on some old nag that won't go faster than a walk."

"Oh, Mama," said Dimity in mortification.

Alistair was quite amused. Since he had promised to be nice to the child, he thought he would see if he couldn't teach her how to deal with that dragon of a mother. He had learned how to cope with just that kind of smothering affection at an early age. And it would be rather fun to tease Margaret. That smirk on her face could only mean that she thought he was already falling for this little beauty. Let her assume what she would then. Her eventual disappointment might teach her a lesson, at last, about the peril of interfering in his life.

At the conclusion of dinner Margaret announced that she had invited several local ladies to a luncheon the next day to meet her guests. "The vicar's daughter is a charming girl and just your age, Miss Farnsworth. Since her cousin, Miss Regina Cressley, is visiting here, I included her too. She is an interesting person, a businesswoman from Manchester. You will enjoy talking to her, Bella. She is quite—er—original." Margaret was pleased with the thought of Miss Cressley's presence the next day. She would take one look at Dimity and head back for Manchester in defeat.

But the object of all Margaret's schemes declared at first that she had no desire to have luncheon at the priory, though one stricken look from Celia had melted her resistance. Celia obviously needed moral support in her first excursion into society since her engagement was broken. Her initial mood of hectic gaiety had quickly turned to a depressing gloom. Even Stephen Thwait's attentive wooing did nothing to lighten her spirits. Celia was not the same content individual she was two weeks ago, and Regina was feeling responsible. She had rushed down to help, and now her cousin's happiness lay in a million little pieces. It was in the hope of comforting Celia that Regina lingered in the small village, but it was something else entirely that sent her walking up the lane to the priory.

The day was warm, and the sun on her neck

had Regina wishing she had left her hair up in its accustomed knot. Celia had gone a step farther this time and had styled her cousin's hair in curls that cascaded down her back. It seemed horribly juvenile, but was a small price to pay if it diverted Celia from her gloom. Regina had even allowed her to trim one of her dresses with rows of lace on the sleeves and neck. Celia declared it to be wonderfully becoming, but Regina professed that she was only wearing it to compliment the creator. Such fine needlework ought to be shown off.

The imposing butler at the priory ushered them out to the garden when they arrived, where a number of wrought-iron tables and chairs were grouped picturesquely on a flagstone terrace. Everyone was dressed elegantly for this auspicious occasion, as it was not every day that Miss Margaret Debenham invited the ladies of Grantly to socialize with her.

Even Mrs. Dawlish, not terribly happy to be meeting Celia in public since her break with Tom, passed muster in a blue lawn dress with no excessive draperies that might trip her up. Celia gave her a poignant look before hurrying over to her hostess. Regina followed more slowly.

"Dimity, my sweet," Margaret cooed, "is there room next to you for Celia? Miss Cressley, I'm sure you will find it much more comfortable here, next to me. The younger set sometimes feels constrained when an older lady is thrust betwixt them." She placed Regina strategically across from the two girls so she could not fail to observe the full potency of Dimity's ethereal loveliness. It was only when Regina sat down that Margaret noticed her exceptional toilette.

That dress was simply a disaster. And those curls. . . . A woman of her years ought to know better than to try and compete with youth. Margaret prided herself on being a shrewd judge of character, and Miss Cressley's startling change in appearance only verified her suspicions. The woman was after Alistair, no doubt about it.

Celia, whose handiwork had elicited this criticism, was quite pleased that Regina was looking her age for once. The others, too, shared Celia's admiration for the charming Miss Cressley, for even though Dimity was the guest of honor, it was Regina who provided the lively conversation. Dimity seemed to have nothing to say, as Mrs. Farnsworth answered all questions for her. Soon no one directed any conversational gambit to the girl unless they wanted to hear from the mother again.

Lobster patties, cucumber sandwiches, and pink-and-blue iced petits fours were passed around by two maids while Margaret poured tea from a large Georgian tea service. Mrs. Farnsworth's plate was still full when she reached for yet another cake, but Dimity, who had not said a word, only toyed with a corner of her bread.

Regina, in kindly persistence, tried to draw the girl out. "How long will you and your mother be staying in Grantly, Miss Farnsworth?" she asked.

Dimity blushed in confusion and looked at her mother for help. Mrs. Farnsworth swallowed her large mouthful in haste and said rather thickly, "A fortnight, I think."

"Oh, at least two weeks, Bella," Margaret burbled. "Alistair would be so disappointed if you didn't. He is so enchanted with Dimity." Margaret smiled benignly on the gathering while the women assimilated this bit of news.

Regina wanted to laugh out loud at the absurdity of this bird-brained child interesting a man like Lord Grantham. Margaret must have looked far and wide to find her. Regina could imagine Tristam Barclay's reaction to "Dimwitty" Farnsworth. He would, no doubt, appreciate her immensely. But Alistair? Never. What Barclay would take pleasure in using as a butt for his humor, the earl would find pitiful. The child couldn't hold a conversation with a half-wit, much less a man of intelligence. No wonder Alistair was off hiding somewhere. Regina derived a sadistic pleasure at the thought of him stuck with her at dinner each night. As for Mrs. Farnsworth, the fastidious Miss Debenham must be regretting her presence already. Why, the woman had consumed at least six sandwiches, putting her hostess to the blush.

"Are you for women's suffrage, Miss Cressley?" piped up the gentle voice of Lady Telford, a white-haired dowager who lived with her widowed daughter on the outskirts of the village.

"I am, at least in principle. Why do you ask?"

124

"Margaret said you run your family's firm, and quite successfully too. The example of women succeeding in a man's field is liberating, I feel. My daughter, Mrs. Eliot, is much concerned with women's rights."

"Perhaps she knows my great-aunt, Penelope Wingarten."

Lady Telford smiled in delight at hearing the name. "I've heard her speak. An extraordinary woman. I had to stretch myself to take in all that she was saying. But with that example in your family, you must be working for the Cause. You young women will derive the benefit from a change in the law."

Regina shook her head doubtfully. "I have done nothing but sympathize. But frankly, it seems the movement is at a standstill. Who knows if even the next generation of women will have the privilege of participating in government?"

Mrs. Eliot, a slender, well-dressed brunette, came over to join the conversation. Sitting by her mother, she leaned forward. "Some of us feel it is time for a change in tactics. What do you think, Miss Cressley?"

"Well, I rather favor open-air rallies to bring our message to the general public," Regina said with a teasing glance at her hostess.

"Miss Cressley, I thought I convinced you that they are self-defeating," Miss Margaret exclaimed.

"Now, Margaret, how can you say so?" Lady Telford interrupted. "Catherine, dear, tell them what happened in Oxford when you addressed the Women's Social and Political Union."

"It was quite exciting. The other organizers and I felt it was successful, though I was hit by a rotten egg. The tomatoes, fortunately, all fell short."

Celia's eyes widened at that. "How shocking!" she gasped. "Did you faint?"

"Not at all," Mrs. Eliot responded calmly. "I ignored the incident and finished my speech. Some students in the crowd dealt with the rowdy element by hustling them away. Even some of the men shouted 'hurrah' when I finished, but whether they approved of my argument or my spirit, I'm not quite sure."

Miss Debenham sniffed eloquently. "It's disgraceful that you allow Catherine to expose herself in such vulgar and dangerous exhibitions, Hetty."

"I'm proud of her," Lady Telford responded with a fond look at her daughter. "Courage is always admirable in my opinion. I think even her father would approve if he were alive today."

Mrs. Eliot gave her mother's hand a quick squeeze. It was easy to see that these two women understood and cared for each other in a way few mothers and daughters achieve.

"And was this in a hall?" Regina asked curiously.

"On the green. The crowd grew enormously from casual passersby. That is the advantage of out-of-doors events. When we schedule a lecture in a rented hall, we find ourselves speaking to a few earnest ladies, while the rest of the world ignores us as a crackpot minority. We have to bring the message to everyone."

The conversation was getting out of hand, and Margaret intervened. "I hope Miss Farnsworth does not get the wrong impression from you ladies. Women's suffrage is serious business. And as for staging a rally on our own village green, I hope all of you realize how disruptive that would be."

"I missed that one," Catherine Eliot said with a laugh. "Not your idea, Miss Margaret, I take it?"

"Not at all. Miss Cressley's."

"Interesting." She studied Regina thoughtfully. "Your name would be a great drawing card here, Miss Cressley. If you would speak, I would be happy to organize a bang-up rally."

Regina declined regretfully, for the idea was tempting. It was impossible, though, since she would not be there long enough to involve herself in such an affair. Besides, Regina had other things on her mind. This flirtation with Alistair was proving most diverting. Poor man, he was being attacked on the home front now, but in this battle Regina was only a cheering spectator. Margaret Debenham's reason for inviting Dimity Farnsworth was amusingly obvious. No one could have missed the heavy-handed insinuations that the girl was here on the earl's account, and Regina had caught every conscious look that Margaret had thrown her way. Word must have gone around this small village that Lord Grantham had

been dallying in the woods with the vicar's unprincipled niece, stirring Miss Margaret to action.
There was no doubt of the outcome, of course.
Not that Miss Cressley was interested in the earl
for herself, but this pathetic little bore, despite
her blue blood and violet eyes, didn't stand a
chance.

CHAPTER EIGHT

"A ball? How extraordinary."

"Yes, isn't it exciting?" Celia's voice held none of the apathy that had marked her demeanor lately. "Shall we go?"

"As if we would dream of missing it! But what to wear? I can't go in my brown suit."

That typically feminine question was irrefutable proof that the steadfast Miss Cressley had yielded at last. The drab severity that she had cultivated over the years was tossed overboard with scarcely a regret. Of course, Regina told herself that she was only allowing Celia the delight of playing dress-up dolls, but there was a certain pleasure in it for the independent Miss Cressley too. Alistair had expressed admiration—no, captivation with a more fashionably dressed Regina; and while she pretended indifference, his attentions were having a profound effect. That afternoon in the woods had been the culmination of three weeks of verbal sparring, and the outcome, though highly improper, had left Regina in a state of flattered expectation. She had no intention of succumbing to the earl's outrageous appeal, but she wanted the thrill of hearing it repeated. Regina ignored the inconsistency of her attitude as she wondered if he would attempt to make love to her in the priory gardens. He seemed to have a penchant for the out-of-doors.

The news that the Debenhams were giving a ball swept through Grantly with the speed of a fire storm, and those poor souls who had been omitted from the guest list were thrown into despair. Mrs. Clarke had it on good authority from her niece Kate, kitchen maid at the castle, that Mrs. Thwait was reduced to tears at the realization that they were among the uninvited.

Meanwhile the staff at the priory grumbled as they bustled about. Lady Margaret was expecting miracles if she thought all could be prepared properly at such short notice. Yet, despite the last-minute rush, the priory was crowded with elegantly gowned ladies and black-tailed gentlemen on the appointed evening, all quite determined to extract the maximum enjoyment from such a rare event.

The ball was being declared a grand success when Regina entered the room on her uncle's arm. Celia stood on his other side, her porcelain beauty revealed in a pale yellow gown with blue ribbons. But it was Regina who drew all eyes. Dark brown curls were piled in careless profusion atop her head, while a black-beaded collar encircled her long throat. Hundreds of hand-sewn bugle beads rimmed the daring plunge of the bodice, and the soft, gray silk gown fell in shimmering folds to the tips of her black satin slippers. It was a provocative ensemble, but no one denied that Miss Cressley carried it off with a haughty grace. If only the two cousins knew that Celia's skillful fingers had fashioned this masterpiece out of what had been a good dress of no particular distinction, it was indeed a success.

Miss Margaret greeted her guests from the vicarage with every evidence of warmth. She had reason to be pleased with the evening so far. Her floral arrangements had turned out particularly well. Roses and trailing leaves fell to the floor in artful disarray, suggesting a bower. The caterers, too, had outdone themselves with an assortment of dishes to tempt the most jaded palate, and a twelve-piece orchestra, hidden behind a screen of potted palms, filled the house with music. It was an extravagant and gala affair, but most worthwhile, as her plan was moving smoothly to its appointed conclusion.

Alistair had shown a decided interest in the exquisite Miss Farnsworth since she had arrived. And this evening, without neglecting his other guests or altering in any way his usual bland good manners, he had given that extra degree of attention to his beautiful houseguest that convinced his sister of his smitten heart.

Nevertheless Margaret was far from pleased at Miss Cressley's appearance in a shockingly fast gown that revealed far too much of what could only be called a passable figure. Really, the woman was a menace.

But for Regina, the night augured well, commencing in a dance with Alistair, who was in high spirits as he twirled her around the floor in an athletic version of the waltz. Afterward the queue lined up to partner the dashing Miss Cressley with breathless regularity. It wasn't until almost an hour later that she had a chance to speak to the earl again. This time he met her at the punch bowl.

"Has anyone told you yet that you look ravishing?"

"Of course. Dozens."

"Then I suppose you will litter up the floor with a score of broken hearts tonight. Miss Cressley would be appalled at that callousness, Ginny my love."

"Then let's not tell her."

Alistair took her hand. "Is she vanquished forever?"

"Oh holiday, shall we say." Regina's talent in the art of flirtation was rusty with disuse, but if the earl's response was any indication, she could still manage creditably. He should be asking her to take a stroll in the garden with him any time now. "Where have you been these past days, my lord?" she teased, rapping him lightly on the arm.

"I did call one afternoon with Dimity, but you were out."

That answer was slightly deflating, but at least he had tried to see her. Having the Farnsworths as houseguests must be trying him sorely. "Yes, we found your card. What a shame we missed you." Then, to draw the response she wanted, "How are you enjoying your visitors? Miss Farnsworth is a lovely girl, isn't she?" Regina laughed up at him, expecting verification that he too found Dimity as dull as she was beautiful.

But Alistair did not play up. "Yes, she is, but terribly shy. Perhaps you might befriend her; the art of conversation comes easily to you."

"What? I imagine she is every man's dream of perfection just as she is, beautiful and silent," Regina said a touch spitefully. So he felt sorry for that tongue-tied nonentity. She didn't. Any girl who looked like Miss Farnsworth needed no pity.

The earl smiled perfunctorily. "She only lacks self-confidence. Dimity has never had a chance against that mother of hers."

Regina was regretting that she had brought up the subject of "Dimwitty" Farnsworth. It was obvious that Lord Grantham, as always, was ready to champion the underdog, but she did not want to waste the evening discussing downtrodden females. As far as that went, Regina, like so many strong people, had little patience for more timid souls.

She gave Alistair a coquettish glance from under her lashes. "Thank you for the flowers you sent over to the vicarage. White roses are my favorite." That should have elicited a smile, at least, if not a leer, but Lord Grantham missed the implication. Evidently he had forgotten their conversation in the castle rose garden.

"I'm glad you like them. Jenner, our head gardener, did a nice job with the corsages this time. Of course, I didn't know what colors all the ladies were wearing, so I told him white would be suitable for everyone."

Involuntarily, Regina glanced around the room. Odd she hadn't noticed that everyone was wearing white flowers, though some were gardenias, and some were carnations. She pressed her lips together. So much for her great expectations. There was nothing more intense in Alistair's eyes tonight than admiration. Had she somehow misunderstood? Was she placing too much significance on that encounter in the woods? The next dance was beginning, and she had time only for one troubled look at him before her waiting partner whisked her away.

Admiral Bulfinch was a long-time friend and neighbor of the Debenhams'. Part of his pleasure in this acquaintance was in the rowdy arguments he had with Lord Grantham on the subject of the House of Lords. Bulfinch, like Debenham, a Liberal, was opposed to that venerable institution, asserting that the peerage was a relic of the past and should be abolished. Why should men have political power because their great-grandfather was a rogue, he'd ask. Since Grantham was in government service prior to his elevation to the earldom, the admiral forgave him privately, but subjected his friend to long-winded tirades on the subject nevertheless.

Tonight he was willing, for once, to forego a friendly harangue with the earl, as other, more exciting possibilities presented themselves. One of them was the attractive Miss Cressley. As Admiral

Bulfinch could testify, there wasn't another woman in the room to compare with her, especially if one were in the unique position of being able to peer down the front of her dress. Being short does have its advantages, the admiral decided sometime during the beginning steps of the mazurka.

"I say," he commented to the top row of bugle beads. "This is a capital party, what?"

Regina drew herself up as straight as she could. "Indeed."

"Care to inspect the gardens with me?"

"I think not."

Deuced dull creature for such a showy dresser, he thought. "Go to Parliament much?"

"I beg your pardon?"

"The visitors' gallery. Don't you watch from there?"

"No, I'm afraid not."

"Hummph. Got my own seat, you know. Stupid bunch."

"Parliament?"

"No, the ushers. Always trying to put me in the back. I'm an admiral, I tell them. That does the trick. Had my own ship, you know. Ever been on a man-o'-war?"

"Would you believe, not once in my life."

"Shame. Ladies always find it romantic. Ever had champagne drunk from your shoe?"

"I don't think so," Regina said faintly.

"Did it on my ship once. Party before going

ashore. Some actress from the Gaiety. Drunk as a lord."

"Oh, dear."

"You've led rather a sheltered life, haven't you, missy? That's what comes of keeping girls at home. Ought to see the world, I say. Well, thank you for the dance."

He bowed smartly, clicked his heels together, and led Regina back to her chair. Comely enough, but cold as a fish, he opined to himself.

Regina wiped her forehead with a lace-trimmed handkerchief and watched his rolling gait across the dance floor. A bothersome gadfly, the admiral, but harmless if one could forgive him his voyeurism. That was the way with most men; they loved eyeing the merchandise, but that women had hearts and minds as well as an interesting assortment of bumps and curves was pretty much ignored. Of course, Alistair was far more perceptive. He would never be taken in by mere window dressing. Yet Regina couldn't keep her eyes from straying to the corner where Alistair was talking to Miss Farnsworth.

Later Celia, too, became engaged in the unrewarding task of conversing with the guest of honor. "Are you enjoying your stay, Miss Farnsworth?"

"Oh, yeth."

Even the talkative Celia was having problems with this conversation. "Isn't Lord Grantham simply wonderfully handsome for such an old man?"

she asked confidingly, in a last-ditch effort to elicit some sort of response.

Dimity blushed and cast down her eyes. "I don't know," she whispered faintly.

Celia gave her a scornful look. "You hadn't noticed, I suppose?" Luckily two young men who had been hovering in the background came forward to ask the girls to dance, and Celia escaped with a sigh of relief. She had decided that Dimity was "wet," a damning term in her lexicon.

It was only as she danced away in the arms of a young naval lieutenent that Celia spotted Tom Dawlish in the doorway. He was not alone.

Margaret also frowned in irritation at the late arrivals. She prided herself on having perfect manners, but her smile was strained when Tom Dawlish sauntered in with that gate crasher. Barclay's name never came within smelling distance of her guest list.

Tom made no pretense of politeness, but leaned against a wall and stared sulkily at Celia as she danced and chatted prettily. He wasn't quite sure why he had decided to flaunt convention by showing up with Tristam in tow, but in his burgeoning attempt at independence, it seemed an appropriately defiant move. Everyone appeared satisfyingly put out with him, and it fed his sense of ill-usage that not one person in the room had approached him at all. Tristam was having no trouble mixing with the slightly surprised guests and making himself quite at home at the buffet tables, but Tom was finding that irreverence took some getting used to. He couldn't manage Tristam's cool amusement at all the raised eyebrows, so he had to content himself with baleful looks at Celia whenever he caught her eye. At least he could make her feel as uncomfortable as he felt.

The poor girl tried hard to ignore Tom's unrelenting gaze, but her nerves were gradually cracking under the strain, and soon she longed for nothing so much as an end to the evening and the chance to escape.

The squire was furious at his son's behavior, but when a few well-chosen words in the boy's ear produced nothing but a mulish expression on Tom's face, the much put-upon father retired to the comfort of the punch bowl. Emboldened by three glasses of the potent drink, he then made a sudden and perhaps foolhardy decision. Looking remarkably like a bull in evening clothes, he lurched across the room and invited Barclay to accompany him into the earl's study down the hall. Shutting the door behind him, the squire paused to gather his thoughts.

Barclay waited coolly for an explanation as Mr. Dawlish regarded him with marked distaste.

"Mr. Barclay, I believe you consider yourself my son's friend."

"Certainly the reverse is true, but I must admit that I have found him pleasant company for a country lad."

"Faugh! What insolence! Then am I right in assuming that the attachment is on my son's side, and that you could tolerate, shall we say, the severance of your relationship?" the squire asked with heavy irony.

"One hopes that one will meet life's disappointments with a gentlemanlike calm."

Enraged, yet encouraged by that insufferable answer, the squire turned away. It would not do to antagonize the man unnecessarily. With an effort he went on, "Perhaps you are aware of the fact that I find you a bad influence on Tom. I would prefer that he did not continue to give you his . . . friendship."

"And Tom has been deaf to your arguments. Well, of course. It is scarcely to be wondered at," Barclay said with irritating smugness.

"I'm a blunt man, Mr. Barclay, so I ask you straight out. Will you leave my son alone? Drop him? I am willing to pay you for the inconvenience. Say two thousand pounds."

"Can there be a price to everything in these degenerate times? Even friendship? I confess, you shock me, Squire." He smiled suavely.

"You may be shocked, Tristam, but I am not." Tom was standing in the doorway, his face white with fury. "Father believes all things are for sale, and that all things are permitted him."

"Tom, listen to me, boy!" The squire held out an imploring hand, but his son ignored it.

"Come on, Tristam. This party is becoming a bore."

Barclay met the helplessly angry expression in the squire's eyes with a shrug. "You see how it is," he said with a sudden flash of kindness before following Tom from the room.

Miss Margaret watched Dimity's progress around the floor on the arm of a neighbor with satisfaction. "The child is a great success. She never lacks for partners."

"She is doing very well," her mother agreed complacently. "I'm very grateful, Margaret. She needed this opportunity to learn how to get on before we go into town this fall. She's a good listener, at least. I've drummed that into her. By the by, who is that man in the velvet jacket? The one going out the door? See, he's waving at you."

"He must be leaving, but I am not going to say good-bye. So rude, these young people!" Margaret watched disapprovingly as Barclay and Tom Dawlish made their farewells to Alistair. "Really! Did you see that, Bella? He kissed his fingers to me!"

"Who is he?" Bella breathed.

"Some second-rate poet who had the temerity to show up uninvited. At least he has the good sense to leave early. He and Tom Dawlish have been very thick since he bought a cottage in Grantly. If the Dawlishes weren't such good friends, I'd speak to the squire about his son's manners. He knows how select I am. A man of that ilk has no place in decent society."

"You mean he isn't a gentleman?" Bella asked.

Margaret raised one supercilious eyebrow. "As to that, there's nothing wrong with his family, but

I don't approve of his morals. He said some very shocking things in my presence." Bella had the good fortune to have them detailed into her receptive ear.

The two ladies had exhausted the subject of Mr. Barclay when Regina danced by. "Did you say Miss Cressley was the vicar's niece? The dress she's wearing is singularly inappropriate. How can her uncle countenance such . . . exposure?" Bella asked in a shocked whisper.

"Disgusting, isn't it? She probably bought it in Paris; she's very wealthy. Owns several mills in the Midlands. Such décolleté is absurd on a thin stick of a woman, don't you agree?" Margaret said enviously.

"Oh, absurd," sighed Bella, whose ample bust strained the magenta bodice of her satin gown.

It had not taken Bella Farnsworth long to fathom the reason for Margaret Debenham's insistent invitation to spend a few weeks at the priory. Margaret was clearly terrified that her brother was on the verge of making a fool of himself over Miss Regina Cressley and hoped that Dimity would distract him sufficiently to avert the tragedy. Bella was shrewd enough to realize that a child like Dimity would be far less trouble as a sister-in-law than the formidable Miss Cressley. No doubt Miss Margaret would continue to function as the earl's political hostess if Dimity became his countess, but Mrs. Farnsworth was not terribly keen on the idea of her daughter taking second place. The prospect of marrying into the

Debenham family was not as appealing as it had once seemed. Dimity might easily do better once she was launched into society. Why, every man here tonight had his eyes on her. Countess of Grantham had a nice ring to it, but a girl like Dimity needn't rush her fences.

Happily, Margaret was unaware of her friend's ambitious thoughts, or she might have been deflected from the critical business of keeping a prudent eye on Miss Cressley. The woman was capable of making a brazen push for Alistair's attention right under her nose.

Regina saw Alistair across the room several times after that, but was unable to catch his eye. After all, a host has certain duties to perform, she allowed. Besides, she had been well occupied keeping an eye out for Celia and enjoying herself in the process.

But when it was time for supper, Regina positioned herself conspicuously by an open French door and looked out into the Japanese-lantern-lit garden. He couldn't fail to see her there. In fact, she wouldn't be surprised if he was tempted to inspect the geraniums before adjourning to the buffet tables. Of course, she would be very cool and refuse him—not the supper, just the interlude prior to that.

She heard a step behind her and turned slowly.

"Miss Cressley, I must speak to you."

Regina regarded Mrs. Dawlish with raging impatience. "What is it?"

"Could we go out onto the terrace?" she beseeched.

Regina quickly scanned the crowd still in the ballroom but did not see the earl. She hurried the distraught woman out the open door.

Mrs. Dawlish rubbed her hands together nervously and tugged at the wisps of gray hair that straggled from her collapsing coiffure. Her words were disjointed as her eyes sought Regina's in mute appeal. "I really don't know where to begin. It's all so confusing. But if Tom were happy, his father would not be so . . . at least, Tom might . . . oh, dear."

"Come sit down on this bench, Mrs. Dawlish. You must calm yourself." Regina was thinking of the curious eyes that would immediately associate this strange behavior with Celia and Tom, and there was enough gossip already without adding to it.

Mrs. Dawlish clutched Regina's hand gratefully. "So kind," she murmured. "That's what I told Gerald. That you looked quite kind."

"Gerald? Oh, Squire Dawlish."

"He is drinking far too much, but he's upset, you realize. A quarrel with Tom. But you can fix everything, I know."

Regina was understandably taken aback. "But my dear Mrs. Dawlish, I hardly know your husband. It would be most presumptuous of me to censure his drinking habits. Perhaps the vicar . . ."

"Oh, but you would know what to say. The vicar is only her father. I tried to talk to her, but she looked as though she was going to burst into tears."

"You mean Celia," Regina said in dawning enlightenment. "It's Celia you wish me to speak to. But I'm afraid that's impossible."

Mrs. Dawlish looked as though she were ready to cry. "But you must . . . no one else . . . oh, everything is in such a . . . Miss Cressley, I do not know where to turn."

Regina attempted a brisk tone. "Tom and Celia must work out their own problems. I have interfered too much already, and any further advice on my part would be rejected out of hand. Perhaps they don't suit after all. Tom will get over it in time, and the squire, too, will become reconciled to the situation."

The French doors opened once again, and a flying figure came rushing out. "Oh, Regina, please let us go home. Tom is behaving in such a strange way, and I do not know if I can stand it anymore. Please, get Father and . . ." She broke off in embarrassed confusion as she saw Mrs. Dawlish. "Oh, dear . . ."

"That is all right, Celia," Mrs. Dawlish said with remarkable composure. "I was just leaving. We will speak again, Miss Cressley." She drew herself up with great dignity and reentered the ballroom, leaving both cousins alone on the terrace.

"What did she want?" Celia asked.

"Nothing that is in my power to do. Oh, Celia, I have made a mess of your life."

"That's nonsense, Regina. I don't care what Mrs. Dawlish said to you. Everything that has happened is for the best. You've just helped me to see the truth."

But Regina had heard so many versions of the "truth" lately that she wasn't sure what it was anymore. "Did Tom try to speak to you tonight, insult you in any way?"

"No, but he was horrid. He kept staring at me and screwing up his face in a funny manner. I don't know where he is right this minute; I lost track of him during the last dance. But if he comes back and starts up again, I couldn't bear it. Can we please go home now?"

Regina hated herself for disappointing Celia. "I'm sorry," she apologized, "but Lord Grantham is escorting me to supper." Even in her own ears that was a lame excuse. Miss Cressley did not normally conduct her affairs at the whim of any gentleman, though lately that assurance was less reliable.

Celia was understandably surprised, but for another reason. "Are you sure? I thought I saw him go in with Miss Farnsworth only a few minutes ago."

There was a moment's silence. "I'm not sure of anything just now . . . but if you're ready, I suppose there is no reason to stay."

Absorbed in her own worries, Celia didn't notice her cousin's uncharacteristic hesitation. "I'll go collect Papa, and we can leave," she said in relief. Then she half turned, grateful that Regina should be willing to retire from the scene of her success. "By the way, everyone is in raptures over your dress. I agreed that it was an original, designed by—" Her voice broke. "I suppose I could always become a seamstress. It's doubtful that I'll ever become a wife."

Regina sat down on the marble bench to wait, her disappointment swiftly changing to vexation. "Men!" she muttered scathingly.

CHAPTER NINE

Regina woke with the unpleasant knowledge that the previous night's events needed sorting out. Sitting up in bed with the covers drawn up around her neck, she frowned thoughtfully out the window into a fresh, blue-skied morning. The rest of the house was still abed, but a troubled night's sleep had left Regina anxious for the dawn.

The ball had been a marvel of sumptuous elegance, equal to any held in town, and Margaret Debenham had shown an enterprising zeal in arranging things so quickly. In fact, the affair of Dimity Farnsworth was managed so slickly it rivaled the trick of pulling a rabbit out of a hat. The tiresome Miss Farnsworth had captivated most of the men present. Tom had been too busy fighting with his father and glowering at Celia to notice the guest of honor, and, of course, Tristam Barclay had remained oblivious to her charms. But those were the only exceptions to what was clearly a triumph. Even the vicar had remarked that Miss Dimity was a beautiful child. Naturally, despite what must have been fierce competition, it was the earl who gained the honor of escorting her to supper.

Regina turned around and punched up her pillow with undue force. How absurd to assume that he would reserve that signal honor for herself. Fortunately Celia had been far too distressed to realize just how chagrined Regina felt. If she had used her head, she would have realized that the earl was duty-bound to see that his guest of honor was shown the proper attention. That might have lessened the shock but not the resentment. In the clear light of morning Regina admitted her own foolishness.

She had gone to the priory on a euphoric wave of anticipation. Confident of what? That Alistair would toast her beauty in champagne as suggested by the preposterous admiral? That he would make mad, passionate love to her in the shrubbery while a hundred guests loitered inside? What flummery! Nor could Regina forget the stricken look in Celia's eyes when Tom appeared with Barclay in tow. It was little wonder that she wanted to flee. Smiling sardonically to herself, Regina thought there had been little to choose from between the two women who had retreated ignominiously from the field of battle. The ride home in the vicarage trap was dismally silent. A fine pair they were, to be sure, allowing two quite ordinary men to destroy their peace of mind.

The sound of Mrs. Gatchell in the kitchen gave Regina an excuse to abandon her unrewarding reflections, but when she descended to the breakfast room, the feast of burnt bacon and cold toast left her with no appetite. Celia, coming in just then, still in her wrapper, offered to prepare a fresh meal, but Regina satisfied her empty stomach with two cups of coffee and went off in search of the morning post.

As she expected, a letter from Dottie stared up at her reproachfully. Somehow affairs in Grantly seemed so much more pressing than business problems, and Regina had been ignoring her secretary's pleas that she was needed in Manchester. Even now she slit open the envelope with scant interest.

Cressley Limited
Manchester
July 10, 1895

Dear Miss Cressley:

It may be of little concern to you, but I think it prudent to inform you that the dock-workers in Liverpool are threatening a strike. Since a great deal of our wool is sitting in a warehouse there, it might be wise to move it quickly. Further, the new treadles you ordered do not fit our looms in the South Factory. At the board meeting on Thursday they discussed the feasibility of ordering the additional part needed, but the question was tabled on the chance that you might know how to install it without this extra expense.

Rumors here are growing daily that there will soon be a change in management. I am doing my best to quash them, but your own delayed return is adding fuel to the fire.

Colonel Pucey, who has been making a rare pest of himself ever since you left, just informed me that a third party has made a bid on John Lassiter's shares. I hardly know whether or not to believe the man, but since Mr. Lassiter has written that he intends to lengthen his stay in Italy indefinitely, as his wife is not up to the rigors of the English climate, then perhaps it is true. Do you know who it could be?

Also enclosed, you will find other correspondence that requires your personal attention. I have dealt with all but the most important, but I am unequal to advising the Prime Minister on his investments.

As for myself, I am praying that your cousin will either elope or join a nunnery so you can come back where you belong.

> Faithfully,
> Dorothy Hodgekiss

This new bit of information added a complication that Regina felt in no mood to face. A third bidder on John's shares, and a secret one by all accounts, was a danger she hadn't considered. He couldn't be any worse a threat than Jeremy Thwait, but why was he interested? A small bloc of shares in Cressley Limited, at the price John was now asking, could not tempt anyone as a pure business investment. And fifteen-percent voting power was useless unless coupled with that of a major stockholder like Colonel Pucey or herself. It appeared the game was growing more complicated.

"Miss Regina, you have callers. Miss Celia is asking if you can join her in the drawing room."

With a gesture of impatience, Regina followed the housekeeper down the hall to the parlor where the earl was sitting comfortably on the horsehair love seat. He looked very much the country gentleman this morning, in form-fitting jodhpurs and a cutaway jacket. The other guest was equally smart in a green spencer and a gracefully divided skirt, while her little feet were encased in riding boots that shone like mirrors.

"Miss Farnsworth, Lord Grantham." Regina hid her start of surprise as she nodded coolly to the visitors and made her greeting. "Please convey my thank you to Miss Margaret. We enjoyed the ball immensely. It was thoroughly delightful."

"Oh, yeth. It wath the moth wonderful evening of my life," said Dimity with a grateful look at Lord Grantham, who smiled foolishly at her artless praise.

"And you were the belle of the ball," he replied.

Regina curled her lip at this display of elderly fatuousness. Really, Alistair was carrying it a bit far.

"Lord Grantham ith tho kind," Dimity breathed shyly. "He'th teaching me to ride. I'm thimply terrible, but he is tho patient that I am learning anyway."

"I can imagine." Regina was impressed despite

herself. This was the first time she had heard Dimity speak more than three words in a row. Apparently the earl was having a great influence on the child. Too much, Regina thought. "Lord Grantham rather fancies himself as a Pygmalion, it seems. And you make a lovely Galatea." Regina cast him a look of disdain. "I was always too stubborn to play the part."

Dimity's face assumed its typically vacuous glaze, but the earl shot Regina a frown before turning the conversation away from her. "Celia, you're such an accommodating girl, that I was hoping you might care to join us for a ride around the neighborhood this morning. Young Thwait said that was your intention, so if you'd be kind enough to bear us company, I'll even sport for a picnic at Westover Hill. Stephen should be here shortly, and we can make a party of it. I'm sure the companionship of young people is much more to Dimity's taste than the sole escort of an old man like myself."

"Oh, Lord Grantham, how kind of you," Celia protested. "I'd love to come. Just give me a minute to change. Stephen isn't due until eleven."

"And would you care to join us?" the earl asked Regina, very much, she considered, as an afterthought.

"I'm sorry, but I have a great deal of correspondence that requires my immediate attention."

"Too bad," he commented, as if her presence on the outing would not be sorely missed. "It might blow some of the cobwebs out of your brain."

"My brain is fine, thank you." Regina was furious. No doubt he was quite relieved that he wouldn't be forced to spend an uncomfortable day flitting between his old flirt and his new. "You seem to have blossomed in Grantly, Miss Farnsworth. So much poise and conversation. Are you sure the earl is not giving you lessons in anything more than the equestrian skills?"

"W-What?" Dimity stuttered and looked at the earl, while her lower lip trembled slightly and her vacant eyes pleaded for help.

This time Alistair was clearly outraged. "Miss Cressley is only teasing, I'm sure. She knows full well that I can take no credit for your being your own sweet self, Dimity dear. Pay her no mind. I certainly don't. Ah, Stephen, just in time. Celia will be down in a moment."

Stephen Thwait, entering just at the moment when things had deteriorated to an abysmal low, was clearly delighted to be included in such august company. He was blithely unaware of the strained atmosphere in the room, as his sole object was to ingratiate himself further with the highest ranking nobleman in the neighborhood.

"I say, Lord Grantham, it's awfully decent of you to include me in your plans. Celia, of course . . ." he broke off as he caught sight of Dimity, sitting quietly in the large, wing-back chair. Her confusion at Regina's attack on Lord Grantham was forgotten as her deep violet eyes took in the devastating phenomenom of Stephen Thwait. He was the handsomest man she had ever seen. For a moment Stephen, too, stood in speechless wonder at the fairy-tale vision before him. Dimity blushed prettily as the earl made the introductions.

"Blimy!" was Stephen's first coherent word, giving testimony to his recent heritage. "Celia told me you had a houseguest, my lord, but no one prepared me for such loveliness. Your servant, Miss Farnsworth."

Dimity presented him with a dimpled little hand, over which Stephen bowed gallantly. "I'm very pleathed to meet you," she whispered, enchanting the young man even more by her quaint manner of speech.

It was clearly a meeting of the minds, Regina thought waspishly. She watched them all leave with equal acerbity, allowing only Celia respite from her rancorous thoughts. And she took a grim satisfaction from the sight of Stephen Thwait vying with Lord Grantham for the honor of remounting the timorous Miss Farnsworth on her impassive nag. It was the earl, though, who received the accolade of her peerless smile.

Watching from the window until they were quite gone from view, Regina then turned away to kick at an offenseless footstool. Doddering old fool! He was as incapable of seeing past a pretty face as the next man. But the earl had outsmarted himself this time, Regina thought maliciously. Stephen Thwait was already under the girl's spell and would not scruple to cut out his competition. But poor Celia! Stephen was proving as fickle as Lord Grantham. "Blast Dimity Farnsworth," Regina muttered as she headed back to the desk in the study.

There was Dottie's letter again, untouched and unheeded. Suddenly it seemed the height of idiocy that her secretary should have to recall her to her sense of duty. Where was the Regina Cressley who let nothing stand in the way of her business life?

It was rampant folly, this ludicrous obsession with a man, especially a man who had just insulted her publicly. Never mind that Dimity was the single witness, and she totally without comprehension. The fact was that Regina had allowed this rake . . . this shameless profligate, to seduce her from her life's work. He had distracted her at a crucial moment too. Instead of lolling in the grass and playing the enchantress, she should have been applying herself to business, seeing her bankers, perhaps even traveling to Italy. Regina did not spare herself. It was useless to blame Alistair for telling her some pretty lies and taking advantage of her stupidity. It was her fault for degenerating into a susceptible romantic. Luckily his treachery brought her to her senses in time. It almost took a thunderbolt to awaken her. Regina could almost pity Lord Grantham for his inconsistency. He could have had the inimitable Miss Cressley at his feet, an achievement, indeed. Instead he would spend his days bored to tears by a lisping recital of his perfections. No one could endure hero-worship forever, not even the multitudinally superlative Earl of Grantham. He would weary of it soon and wish for a more astringent partner. Well, too bad. By then Regina would have long forgotten him . . . and his wretched sister.

With a snort of disgust, Regina ripped at the absurd ruffles on the candy-striped muslin gown that Celia had unearthed from some moldy closet. She gave a painful yank at the silly curl that dangled with infantile cuteness over her brow. Enough! It was finished.

Mounting the stairs in a determined rush, Regina charged into her room and pulled the brown suit from the back of the closet. Within moments the offending dress was in a heap on the floor and the ridiculous hairstyle transformed into a familiar topknot. Regina gazed with dour satisfaction at the eminently sensible woman in the mirror. No one would dare trifle with her affections. Miss Cressley of Cressley Limited then marched herself back down the stairs to deal with her correspondence.

But alas for her resolutions to keep her mind strictly on business: Even as she began drafting a reply to Dottie, Mrs. Dawlish was announced. Miss Cressley uttered a mild oath but presented herself dutifully in the front parlor. Mrs. Gatchell's stern look of reproof was the only indication that Regina's outburst had been overheard.

"Mrs. Dawlish, how delightful to see you again. May I offer you some refreshment?"

The good lady fidgeted with the fringe of her shawl and mumbled something about a cup of

jasmine tea. Her agitation was such that Regina
had small hope of saving the collection of minia-
tures on the étagère next to her. She strategically
moved the teapot to the uncluttered table in the
corner by the window. Mrs. Dawlish seemed unaware of her immediate surroundings, as she was
in an advanced state of nervous anxiety. Regina
could have served her beef bouillon in a brandy
snifter and she wouldn't have taken exception to
it.

"Miss Cressley, I pray you can help me . . .
so sure of yourself . . . so intelligent. I could
barely sleep last night. It's been a catastrophe.
The squire is raging, you can imagine . . . and
with Tom gone—oh, it's all so terrible," she wailed.

Regina interrupted impatiently. "What has happened, Mrs. Dawlish? I'm afraid you've lost me."

At that the beleaguered woman became even
more incoherent. "Tom is gone, Miss Cressley.
My husband is furious. He might have apoplexy
. . . his father died of that, you know. It runs
in the family . . . all such excitable people."
On that dire prediction, she promptly burst into
tears.

Regina calmed her finally and made her take a
swallow of tea. Eventually her hiccuping ceased,
too, and she was able to give Miss Cressley a
watery smile.

"I know I'm a silly woman," she said tremulously, "but I can't help feeling that all of this is
my fault."

"You can't blame yourself if Tom and his father

have had a falling out. You'll see how quickly they fall right in again."

"Not this time, Miss Cressley. It's gone too far. After last night Tom will never speak to his father again . . . and my husband is threatening to disinherit him."

Regina felt she was finally making headway. "What happened last night?"

Mrs. Dawlish composed herself sufficiently to tell her story. "You must have noticed. I'm sure it escaped no one's attention that my son brought Mr. Barclay to the ball. He was not invited, and I thought Miss Debenham took the intrusion rather well, as she is usually most direct when displeased. My husband was appalled, of course, and took Tom to task over his impudence. But Tom seems to go his own way when it comes to Mr. Barclay, though I cannot see the attraction, to tell the truth. My son, naturally, took no notice of his father, so the squire may have gone a bit too far when he offered Mr. Barclay two thousand pounds to leave Grantly and never see Tom again."

"What an astute move," Regina applauded. "You are well rid of the man, Mrs. Dawlish, even if the squire's means were rather unorthodox."

"Oh, no, Miss Cressley. If only things had worked out that way. But Tom saw my husband go off with Mr. Barclay, and he followed them. Of course, he overheard everything, and before the man could accept or reject the offer, Tom denounced his father for interfering in his life and insulting a man of Barclay's integrity."

"What a shame he didn't wait a moment before charging in. He might have found it enlightening."

"Then you think Barclay would have accepted? Oh, but it's too late now. Tom raced home and packed his things. This morning we found a note that he had moved into Honeysuckle Cottage. Even his motor car is gone." Mrs. Dawlish regarded Regina hopefully, as if her divine intelligence could conjure up an immediate solution.

"Of course," Regina answered absently, wondering how long Barclay would risk jeopardizing that two thousand pounds. She knew that weighed more with him than the capricious extravagances of a wayward boy, no matter how plump in the pocket. The benefits the squire offered were more stable. Besides, Tom had become an annoyance anyway. Regina noticed how Barclay grimaced painfully when Tom's exuberance got out of hand. If the choice were his, she'd wager that two thousand herself that the great Tristam Barclay would have played that hand very differently. Tom's precipitate action had forestalled him, but the squire should be receiving a visit from the poet very shortly. Regina tried to convince Mrs. Dawlish of this, but the woman would not be consoled.

"It is a judgment on the parent. 'As you sow, so shall you reap,'" she murmured, nodding her head in doleful accord.

Mrs. Dawlish must be referring to her husband's affairs. No doubt they preyed on the poor woman's mind. "I'm sure the squire's transgressions cannot be blamed for this," Regina consoled, although she thought privately that the man should be horsewhipped for the suffering he caused his wife.

"Gerald's sins? Mere pecadillos," Mrs. Dawlish proclaimed with astonishing forbearance for one so ill-used. "No, Miss Cressley, the fault is mine that things have come to this pass. It is my sin that haunts us all."

Mrs. Dawlish spoke with more force than she had yet shown, and Regina suppressed a smile at her dramatics. "Did you overspend your household allowance?"

The woman regarded her with noble tolerance. "I had an affair."

The bald statement was not so much a confession as a timorous reproof that Regina could so underestimate the lady. Nevertheless it was a shocking admission, and Regina marveled at Mrs. Dawlish's boldness in revealing it. "My dear lady, surely . . ."

"I never thought I'd be able to say it, but you are a persuasive confidante, Miss Cressley."

Regina accepted this unwarranted tribute with mixed emotions. "But the squire—" she began.

"Oh, Gerald has these little romps with the maids, but I blame myself for it. I betrayed him far more terribly, don't you see? He deserves whatever bit of happiness he can snatch. Our marriage is a sham."

Regina was open-mouthed. Mrs. Dawlish was contradicting all her preconceived notions that the woman was no more than a pathetic creature, victimized by a tyrannical and unfaithful husband. It appeared that Mrs. Dawlish had unplumbed depths to her, though Regina was oddly reluctant to delve further.

But once started, the squire's wife had every intention of finishing. She reverted to her usual timidity, though her story was far from demure. "It's a relief to finally admit it," she said, dropping her napkin on the floor and putting her tea cup on the very edge of the table.

Regina ignored the napkin but moved the cup to a safer position. "Who was it?" she asked, consumed with curiosity despite feeling a great dread that somehow the unfolding tale would affect her as well.

"Well, it began when I had this small problem after Aggie married and moved to India. I was dreadfully down, out of sorts, and I couldn't eat. Gerald was horribly worried about me, quite frantic, in fact. So he took me to a health spa in Switzerland for a cure, so to speak, to buck me up. Poor Gerald. He stayed a month, and then I sent him home. He didn't want to go, of course; that was what was so wicked of me. I was really quite well by then, except still too thin. But I wanted him gone. You see, 'it' had already begun."

Regina was fascinated despite herself. "By 'it,' do you mean the affair?"

Mrs. Dawlish pulled a handkerchief from her sleeve and dabbed at her eyes. "I stayed six months, and they were the happiest of my life. Klaus begged me to divorce Gerald, but in the end, I couldn't bring myself to do it, so I came home again. Since that time, I . . . I haven't been . . . I can't bear for Gerald to . . . touch me. Poor man. I think he knows, but he's never said a word."

There was a small silence. "Well," Regina said inadequately. "I can understand your guilt, but it has nothing to do with Tom and Celia."

"It does, Miss Cressley. If my husband weren't so unhappy about me, he'd have handled the situation quite differently. It's all been too much for him. And I don't want to see him hurt anymore. I know he seems strong, but most of it is bluster. He's really very confused. He thinks Tom is in danger of turning . . . funny. It's nonsense, I know, but, Miss Cressley, please won't you talk to Celia? She has only to say one word, and Tom will be begging her forgiveness. He is as pig-headed as his father but just as loyal. Only, she must make the first move."

It was listening to a similar appeal that had precipitated all the trouble to begin with, and Regina felt she had sufficiently learned her lesson not to interfere again. But Mrs. Dawlish only wanted everyone put back in their proper place again, and since it was Regina who disarranged things, it was up to Regina, it seemed, to sort all the little chess pieces into their correct positions once more. Despite her reservations, and the doubtful chance of success, she promised Mrs. Dawlish to give it her best efforts, and the woman departed with newfound hope.

It was uncomfortably clear that the squire's wife considered Miss Cressley a fount of wisdom. If only it were true. Regina knew that she had made a hash of Celia's life as well as her own. The actions of the Earl of Grantham had shown her the folly of diverging from the path of common sense. But perhaps there was still hope that Celia's plight could be remedied.

Squaring her shoulders, Regina returned to the unfinished letter to Dottie.

. . . so send this figure off to that fool John Lassiter and tell him this is my final offer. As for Celia's wedding plans, I expect to have them organized shortly. The happy event will take place in August as scheduled. I hope to be back at my desk by the end of the week. Until then, keep up the good work.

> Yours truly,
> Regina Cressley

P.S.: Do not read any more correspondence from the PM. That is strictly confidential.

CHAPTER TEN

After lunch Mr. Cressley left for the priory library, as usual, to prepare for the next day's sermon, while Mrs. Gatchell was dispatched to the post office with a wire to Regina's banker and a special delivery letter to Miss Hodgekiss. Regina was left alone in the house. She paced the floor in the study, stewing over the morning's revelations.

She had been a fool; she freely acknowledged it. The first mistake had been in involving herself in Celia's problems. Regina had rushed into a situation that needed a great deal of delicacy and had muddled up quite a few lives. She was determined to set one straight, at least. Celia shouldn't have to suffer because her cousin was a cocksure idiot. But the first mistake had led to the second, and that wasn't going to be as easy to fix.

What had made her think that Alistair was different from other men, a unique and marvelous person who actually understood and appreciated her independence? Instead he was just a rake who played destructive games with the nearest available female. Regina had believed every pretty lie, every flattering word, while telling herself she was remaining cool, in control. What a joke! She had been as gullible as any affection-starved spinster, even to imagining that she looked attractive in those absurd clothes. How Margaret must have laughed at Miss Cressley's attempt to play femme fatale! It was insidious, horrible, to lose all sense of proportion, to stop thinking, stop standing on her own feet. She had practically relinquished her identity in trying to please Alistair. At least she had recovered her sanity now. And if she were a little bruised in the region of the heart, she would no doubt heal shortly.

Impatiently, Regina walked into the front parlor and sat down at the piano bench. In a desperate attempt at humor, she told herself that her "savage breast" could stand some soothing. The rendition was not particularly musical, but the crashing chords of Liszt's "Hungarian Rhapsody" were satisfactorily loud, so it was no wonder that she did not hear the knock at the front door or the firm footsteps in the hall.

"Regina, I want to speak to you."

Whirling around, Regina stared at the object of her inflamed resentment. "What are you doing here?" she asked rudely, frowning up at him.

"What is the matter with you? Your behavior was appalling this morning. Dimity was nearly in tears when she left!"

"Poor Dimity was hurt?" Regina laughed mockingly. "How dreadful. Pray ask her forgiveness for me."

Alistair was looking at her in grim surprise. "Has something happened? Why are you dressed like that?"

Regina looked down at her tweed skirt. "You don't approve? Sorry, Alistair. Masquerades can be kept up only so long, I'm afraid," she said with a wintry smile. "You haven't answered my question yet. Why aren't you still feeding grapes to sweet Dimity? Weren't you going on a picnic with her?"

"The picnic is over, and Dimity and Celia are having a comfortable visit at the priory. I wanted to see you."

"Really? I can't imagine why," Regina returned, rising from the piano bench. "May I offer you some refreshment?"

"You can't imagine why?" he echoed. "Regina, what has upset you?"

"Oh, nothing," she said shakily. "It's just that I've probably lost my chance to buy Lassiter's shares."

"Is that all? Why, you don't have to worry about that. I . . ."

"Is that all?" Regina blazed at him. "I suppose that you're happy I've forfeited everything that matters to me! And it's your fault too."

The earl asked with restraint, "Would you mind explaining just exactly why it's my fault?"

"Because you distracted me from my business. I was so busy being flattered into making a fool of myself that I forgot about the most important thing in my life. I was thinking about you instead. Oh, go away, why don't you. Go cuddle Dimity. I'm sure you make a perfect couple." Regina said the last wearily, turning her back on him.

The truth was dawning at last, but Lord Grantham took no satisfaction from it. "Are you jealous? Good God, how can you be?"

"I wonder myself," she answered moodily. "If you prefer that empty-headed little doll to me, so be it. Really, Alistair, you are making a sad mistake. The prospect of that mother-in-law alone should bring you to your senses."

"You have me married to her already, I see."

If Regina had not been so absorbed in her own grievances, she would have seen that Alistair was very angry by now. "Margaret is thrilled, of course," she went on sarcastically. "She evidently knows you a great deal better than I do. I imagined that you were too fine, too intelligent, to fall for such an obvious game."

"Sit down and be quiet," he snapped. "I've listened long enough to this absurd tirade. It's my turn now."

"Tirade?" Regina queried hotly. "When I think how you've trifled with my affections . . ."

"My God, woman, will you shut up?" he roared.

Regina sat down on the horsehair sofa, and with a dangerous glint in his eye the earl sat beside her. "You've made a few accusations, and I think I deserve a chance to answer them."

"You owe me no explanation, my lord," she said frigidly, turning away from him to stare straight ahead.

"You'd try the patience of a saint," he muttered. "The fact is, you're a damned contrary female. You told me to my face you wanted nothing to do with me that day in the woods. 'No affair, my lord, and certainly not marriage!' It might trammel your precious freedom, by God. So what is it to you if I engage myself to fifty juvenescent morons?"

Regina swallowed hard and stole a look at the furious man beside her. "I will not stay here to be sworn at. Your language is unseemly."

"No doubt, but you will listen to me anyway. You say I've trifled with your affections. I'm glad to hear you have them, my dear. I'd begun to think you'd discarded such useless things some time ago."

"And what do you call trying to seduce me? You are a deceiver, Lord Grantham."

"Must you behave as if you were the heroine of some tragic romance?" he said impatiently. "If you will only attempt to be rational, you may recall that it was you who brought up the word *affair*. I am too conventional to dream of seducing such an iron maiden as yourself. My intentions were strictly honorable. Happy, Regina, that you have had a chance to turn me down flat twice?"

Regina looked at him gloomily. "You are fickle, my lord. Poor Dimity will be crying her eyes out."

"Dimity! I was kind to the poor child; I felt sorry for her. Are you so insecure that my mere politeness to a houseguest is taken as proof of an infatuation?" he asked, exasperated. "You can't be that stupid, Regina. The fact is, you're so terrified of making a commitment to me, or anyone, that you've conjured up a romance for me with that child out of whole cloth. If you can tell yourself that I am a rake, a flirt, then you can wriggle back into that safe, emotionless little world you inhabit."

Grabbing her hand, he pulled her over to the mirror. "Look at yourself. See that sour woman? You've distorted yourself, turned into a neuter, so you can pretend to be invulnerable. It's inhuman, but then being human hurts, and Miss Cressley is above such weaknesses. I should have guessed that was where you were headed twelve years ago."

Jerking away, she turned to confront him. "That's quite an argument, Lord Grantham. If I don't want you, then I am unnatural. It must soothe the pride I wounded to think so."

"Have you ever wanted anyone to upset the well-ordered pattern of your life?" he retorted. "How long has it been since you've seen your mother . . . two years? You've shut out everyone who might make demands on you. The only reason you came rushing to Celia's defense was because her cry happened to be your favorite cause. If you could convince her to forget about marriage to an unworthy fellow, it would be proof that independence is worth any price. She would also provide some longed-for company to share your hollow isolation, never mind that she might prefer a nursery full of pink-and-white babies to a life of businesslike sterility."

Alistair's words were cutting, biting into the very fabric of Regina's staunchest beliefs and making them seem selfish, unfeeling. She wanted to lash back at him.

"I hope your brutal attack is some comfort to you, because I find this discussion simply proof that you do not understand me at all. I came to help Celia, and if I was wrong to interfere, as I think I was, it was an honest mistake. I refuse to accept your biased view of my life and my personal relationships. Nothing you can say will make me believe that marriage is a cure for all ills, including loneliness. What kind of instant happiness is there in being an unpaid servant or pampered doll to some demanding male?"

The Earl of Grantham threw up his hands in despair. "You always did talk about marriage in the abstract, as if it were a rare, tropical disease. And you insist on assuming that all men are alike: autocratic like your father, I suppose. That's why you couldn't bring yourself to trust my promises that we could have a different sort of marriage, one of mutual respect and independence."

Regina listened impatiently. "You've always been a dreamer, though I know you meant well when you promised our marriage would be a partnership. But it would never have worked. I wanted to live in Manchester, and even then you were headed for London, anxious to save the world. How could a long-distance wife hostess political dinners? And children! They would have ended my business career rather promptly! We would have done nothing but quarrel, until I capitulated and became a proper wife."

"That's what you've convinced yourself of, anyway."

"The truth is, I couldn't have done what I wanted to do if I had married. No man would have let me put my career first. I had to make a choice, and it was the right one for me."

"Well and good, Regina. You've done what you wanted: achieved success. But is it enough? You said—forgive me for reminding you—that you had been thinking of me these last weeks, forgetting business. Is that true?"

Regina gave him a goaded look. "You know it is. I even dressed to please you. And very amusing it must have been too. You mocked my appearance today, but take a good look, Alistair. It is the real me. The other was just an illusion; she doesn't exist."

"I think she does. Shall we see?" He pulled her close to him, his determined face only inches away. "I understand you very well; I always did. But words don't penetrate that barrier you've built around yourself. You've bottled up your emotions so long you don't even know they're there, but I do."

Regina's voice came out in a frightened whisper. "Don't, Alistair."

"Don't what? Touch the untouchable Miss Cressley? Fight me, Regina. It's what you do best."

His mouth was punishing, his arms a prison she could not escape. There was no tenderness, no affection in his kiss, only a chastening denunciation.

The motionless figure in his arms gave Lord Grantham a feeling of revulsion at his act. He was trying to force Regina to return a love she did not feel. It had only alienated her further from him. He released her and turned abruptly away. "I apologize. That was uncalled for," he said without looking at her.

Regina was in turmoil. She wanted to whip up a white-hot anger at Alistair, but she couldn't. So much of what he said was true. Still, he asked for too much. She wasn't ready to bend to that degree; it might break her altogether. Regina resisted an impulse to throw herself into his arms. They had both said far too many unforgivable things, and she needed time to sort out her confused reactions.

Surprisingly, her voice was steady as she answered. "Don't apologize. But you see how impossible it is? We cannot come to terms on anything."

Unsmiling, he gazed at her for a moment before turning on his heel and leaving her alone in the darkening room.

Dinner that evening was a subdued business. No one had any interest in the overdone roast beef and soggy Yorkshire pudding. Even Celia couldn't seem to summon up her usual concern over Mrs. Gatchell's indifferent housekeeping. She had come back from the priory in a thoughtful mood, only saying that Stephen had joined them during the afternoon for a game of lawn tennis. She didn't add that he had been so busy helping

Dimity improve her game that he had hardly paid any attention to the girl he had professed to be madly in love with only three days before.

Regina picked at her food and wondered how soon her uncle would leave the table so she might finally have a long-overdue talk with Celia.

Arthur Cressley, for once, was keenly aware of the undercurrents that kept both his daughter and his niece from indulging in their normal chatter, and he had the good sense to take his leave as soon as Mrs. Gatchell cleared away the lumpy blancmange. Nothing had been the same since Regina had swooped into their lives, and he, for one, would be glad when she went back to Manchester.

Regina was ready to go herself, but she was determined to settle the question of Celia and Tom first. Despite recent events, Regina was still confident that she could arrange matters, and after dinner she tackled the subject in her usual forthright style.

"Mrs. Dawlish came to see me today, Celia." It had only been that morning, although it seemed a lifetime ago. "Tom has left home."

Celia looked up from her embroidery. "I heard. He moved in with Mr. Barclay."

Regina tried to see some evidence of emotion in that comment, but Celia seemed unperturbed. Regina went on. "His parents are terribly worried. Of course, Tom was forced into the move. The squire practically threw him out of the house."

"Tom and Mr. Barclay will no doubt enjoy the

arrangement. They are two of a kind." Celia delivered this judgment coolly, with no trace of sympathy for the unfortunate Tom or his parents.

"Oh, I don't think so. I imagine this is a very temporary arrangement. Tom couldn't stay at home after the quarrel, and Honeysuckle Cottage is merely convenient. He's probably regretting the move already, and Mrs. Dawlish says the squire is heartbroken. Couldn't you intervene? The old man brought it on his own head, but I do pity him most sincerely."

"Regina, I don't understand you. Why should I interfere? I thought you disliked the squire and Tom, too, for that matter."

"I've changed my mind. The squire is irascible but good-hearted, and I may have been unjust to Tom as well."

"Oh, no," Celia shook her head. "You were right about Tom. He's immature, selfish, unreliable, and I'm sure he's perfectly happy with that rotter, Barclay."

Celia said all this with great conviction, and Regina listened in growing dismay. She had done her work too well. Repairing the fragile web of love and trust was more difficult than she had imagined. It had been torn apart with careless ease; could she reweave the skein?

"Surely you can't be as indifferent as you pretend," she exclaimed. "Don't let pride stand in the way of a reconciliation, Celia."

"If Tom wants to make up our quarrel, then he must apologize to me. But I don't think he wants to. It's quite clear whom he prefers. He cast me off for the sake of his friendship with that creature. Thank goodness I discovered what sort of person he was before I married him."

"Please, Celia! He didn't cast you off. You broke the engagement." Regina was in the difficult position of having to knock holes in her own arguments without losing all credibility. "No man will make an ideal husband until he is taught. And this separation has taught Tom a great deal. He knows that he cannot take you for granted, and that is a step forward. The rest can be safely left until after the wedding."

"After the wedding! How funny. Haven't you heard, Regina? There isn't going to be one."

"There could be, I'm sure. Tom is still here in Grantly, not off in London having a good time. And the way he behaved at the ball certainly suggests that he is very much in love with you. Oh, it was uncomfortable, to be sure, but have you thought how miserable Tom must be? He's proud and stubborn, so he can't beg to come back, but all you have to do is show him the slightest encouragement, and he will be on your doorstep, contrite as you please."

"Regina, you're forgetting everything that happened. If Tom can prefer Barclay to me today, who will take his fancy tomorrow? I don't need a relationship that puts me a long way second to everyone else. I expect a certain loyalty from a husband, and I don't intend to settle for less."

"You can't expect him to make you his entire

world, my dear. Won't you want to have friends, too, perhaps to be active in the Ladies' Guild, or involve yourself in the movement to enfranchise women? Should Tom resent that? Forbid you to participate?"

"Of course not. Those are trivialities. But I would expect him to be jealous if I clearly put another individual relationship before ours."

"And Tom has with Barclay? Are you sure? Maybe you didn't give Tom a chance to show that, as much as he enjoyed and was flattered by Barclay's company, it was you he loved."

"Regina, why are you busy arguing Tom's case? You made much more sense when you advised me to consider well before rushing into a hasty marriage. It was Tom's decision, more than mine, to end our engagement. What happiness would there be for me in conceding to his selfish absorption with Barclay? I'd be a doll, a toy in a fake marriage that was all on his side. My needs wouldn't be considered. I'd be a convenient background, subjugated, silenced, and ignored. You know, I used to feel sorry for you because you never married. It seemed a lonely, sterile life. But now I fully understand and agree with your decision. A woman loses her identity under the guise of a man's protection. She becomes a piece of property, a chattel, to be used at his convenience. No. I'm glad I made the choice I did. It saved me the agony of becoming a wife."

Regina listened to her own words coming from

Celia's mouth, and they sounded trite, the empty rhetoric of self-indulgent deceit. She leaned forward, earnest that Celia should not misunderstand her now. "I said a lot of things a few weeks ago, but I forgot a few things too. I am no one on whom to model yourself. My precious independence has its other side, Celia: loneliness, self-absorption, selfishness. I've achieved a lot, and I'm proud of it. But somewhere in the last few years I also forgot to care about people. And other people matter. I've learned that right here in Grantly. It isn't just a question of whether Tom loves you enough to give up someone for your sake. The other question is whether you love him. If you do, you still have time to salvage happiness for both of you. There's nothing wrong that a bit of compromising on both sides can't mend. Both you and Tom are entitled to a certain amount of freedom. Don't throw away your happiness, my dear. Love is a fragile thing, but infinitely precious when it exists on both sides."

Celia sat silent, but her expression showed no particular softening. Regina had the empty feeling that it was too late; she had achieved nothing.

Celia broke the silence at last. "Darling Regina, don't take it to heart. It's not your fault. Love may be wonderful, precious, as you say. But self-respect is worth even more; you've taught me that. No matter what else we lose, we can go on when we have that." She dropped a light kiss on

Regina's forehead. "And you don't have to reproach yourself about Lord Grantham. He is as faithless as any other man." With that she walked firmly out of the room.

CHAPTER ELEVEN

On Sunday morning Honeysuckle Cottage maintained the Sabbath quiet long after the church bell had rung to summon the village to prayers. It was near noon when Tristam Barclay rang for his manservant and struggled into his brocaded dressing robe. Jenkins, well used to his master's ways, moved silently around the room, offering no superfluity of motion or sound to try the patience of Barclay's sensitive nerves.

Tristam sat passively under Jenkins's ministrations, refusing to open either bloodshot eye while wincing at the scraping razor. The brandy had been potent the night before, and he had indulged himself beyond his usual limits.

The knock at the bedroom door was perhaps not as thunderous as it seemed to the sufferer, but his eyes flew open, and he pointed in silent rage. Although Jenkins moved with incredible speed, he was not swift enough to forestall a repetition of the barbarous thumping. Tom stuck his head in and spoke in good faith. He even moderated his tone of voice. Two nights as Barclay's houseguest had taught him caution.

"Good morning, old chap. I say, is breakfast ready? I've been out for a walk and I'm famished."

"Go away," Tristam enunciated painfully.

Jenkins gave a meaningful nod to the young man. "I'll be along directly to serve breakfast, sir. Just you settle down in the dining room."

"Thank you, Jenkins. Hurry up, will you, Tristam? The morning's gone. As it is, you've missed the best part of the day."

The door closed firmly on the cheery whistle of irrepressible good health, while Barclay groaned softly, his palms held to throbbing temples.

Sometime later Barclay, conventionally dressed except for the silk scarf tucked into the open neck of his shirt, entered the dining room and poured himself a cup of coffee. Tom, who was finishing up a hearty breakfast of eggs, ham, and toast, greeted him pleasantly.

Barclay grimaced. "Softly, please. My head will not stand for conversation at the moment."

"Got a hangover, have you? So sorry. Pater has a cure that works every time. You put a raw egg in a measure of whiskey, beat it up to a froth, and down it one go. I'll have Jenkins bring it presently."

"No," Barclay glared. "No, thank you. Just leave me alone, that's a good chap. Please don't hesitate to eat and run."

Tom's sincere young face registered concern. "Oh, I couldn't go off and leave you when you're feeling so rotten. I'll be quiet though," he offered kindly.

"Thank you," Barclay muttered as he endeavored, with shaking fingers, to drink his coffee.

Tom was as good as his word, and except for the rattling of the paper and a few joyful chortles over the cricket scores, the silence was unbroken in the pleasant dining room for some time. But Tom felt the need to talk. On his long walk this morning he had made quite a stab at examining his life. The fact was, he missed Celia dreadfully. His anger and hurt feelings had kept him from realizing it at first. Now he was bored and unhappy. Of course, she had been wrong, trying to bully him like that, but there must be a way to make her see the error of her ways. She couldn't really care for that jumped-up fool, Stephen Thwait, he told himself. Not his Celia. Slowly, laboriously, Tom had evolved a plan. It needed Tristam's help.

"I say, Tristam, are you feeling better?" Tom ventured at last.

"No," came the short reply.

"Oh, say, how miserable for you! But I could use some words of wisdom. Could you listen to me for a minute?"

Barclay looked wearily across the room. "Promise you'll then shut up and go away?"

Tom grinned. "Word of a Dawlish."

"All right, but make it succinct, if you please."

Tom wrinkled his forehead, trying to sort out his tangled thoughts and chop them down to "succinct." "You know about women, Tristam. I need some help with Celia."

"Celia? You still want her? She is the managing

sort, my boy. I'd thank heaven for a blessed re-
lease."

Tom did not like Barclay's tone and he stiffened
in his chair. "Miss Cressley is a wonderful girl.
High minded, intelligent, too good for me."

"That is the kind of silly thinking that makes
for a long and unhappy life. Love her as much as
you like, but don't put her on a pedestal. The
pedestal will turn out to be your neck."

"Now see here, Tristam, I didn't ask you for
your opinion, only some help in getting her back."

"Shhh, remember my head. Why, it's quite
simple. Go to her and tell her you were wrong.
Say you eschew my company forever. She'll take
you back in a flash."

Tom looked haughty. "I would never do that,"
he exclaimed.

"Actually, that may not be necessary. Jenkins
tells me that Stephen Thwait is moonstruck by the
Debenhams' new houseguest. Wait a few days for
the fact to sink in, and then stop by the vicarage
with some flowers. Your Celia will do the rest.
She'll be too grateful to cavil."

"Stephen prefers that silly Dimity to Celia? I always knew he was an idiot, but how could anyone
be so stupid?" Tom frowned ferociously. "Poor
Celia, d'you suppose she will be hurt?"

"Her pride, at least," Barclay yawned. "But
that's your opportunity."

"I'm not so sure," Tom said. "Celia is not going
to forget that she wants me to drop you. Why
don't you call on her, convince her that she has

nothing to worry about, that we can all be good friends?"

"No."

"Why not? You could charm her in ten minutes, if you tried."

"My dear chap, because I don't care to. Moral women are exceedingly tedious."

"You won't?" Tom asked blankly. "But Tristam, I love her."

"How moving. Nevertheless, I fail to see that it affects me, except to prompt you to return to the parental fold. You did say your visit was to be brief. Put my advice to the test; you won't be disappointed. Nor I," he finished to himself.

"You're awfully cool," Tom said bitterly. "I could almost think you want me to clear out permanently."

"How very dense he is, to be sure!" Barclay said in exasperation. "I was going to be more tactful, but evidently some things have to be spelled out. You no longer amuse me, dear boy, and your presence here at Honeysuckle Cottage has become a shade inconvenient. You are incurably ordinary and have resisted, with all resilience of a rubber ball, my efforts to shape you into a finer form. Take your bags and depart. I wish you bon voyage."

Tom's face had changed colors during this last speech, delivered in a world-weary drawl. "You're joking," he said feebly.

"I never joke before one o'clock on a Sunday." Barclay's mouth pursed into a cruel little smile.

In the act of turning miserably away, Tom stopped. "Pater? He bought you off! It's true, isn't it?"

"Two thousand pounds, boy. A fortune! And if he had waited a week, I would have done it for much less. You are so fatiguingly energetic, child, and never know when your presence is *de trop*. Such a beautiful body, with a mind that is irredeemably commonplace. You are simply not my sort, boy, and you should know it."

Shock and embarrassment mingled on Tom's open countenance as an ugly suspicion dawned. "You don't mean that you are—funny?" he stammered. "Did Pater think that you and I were . . . more than friends?"

"I have no idea what prejudiced and farcical ideas darkened his narrow little mind," Barclay said, smiling in cold amusement at Tom's flustered and scarlet face.

"But you never said . . . or did anything," Tom waved his hands to indicate what was for him unspeakable.

"Of course not," Barclay answered in withering tones. "You were not interested in such a relationship, were you? Well then. I am not generally obtuse, though you are."

Tom was looking at his old friend with all the fascinated disgust that would have been elicited had Tristam changed into a snake before his very eyes. "I don't believe it," he said shakily. "You're just trying to get rid of me. Don't worry; you have. And since I'm so boring, and you've already collected your ghastly fee, I'd better go."

"That's the idea," Barclay said in encouragement.

After Tom's swift and undignified retreat from Honeysuckle Cottage, Jenkins brought his master a restorative glass of wine and a few digestive biscuits.

"You handled a difficult situation well, sir," Jenkins said respectfully.

"Ah, yes. He will go directly to his Celia. We will not see him again."

"Very good, sir. And may I say that the money will come in handy just now. That last little flutter at Epsom left us a bit short."

Barclay turned his eyes on Jenkins in mild surprise. "You believed that I took his father's money? I haven't seen the gentleman since the night of the ball. No, young Dawlish was becoming a bit of a nuisance, so I took steps. When he jumped to that ridiculous conclusion, I allowed him to save face with the fantasy."

"But won't he discover the truth?" Jenkins asked doubtfully.

"Does it matter? But I wager that he will not dare mention the notorious Tristam Barclay to his father, now or ever. I shall send a silver cup to his firstborn. Remind me, Jenkins."

Sunday dinner was just over at the vicarage when the green Daimler pulled into the driveway in a spray of gravel. Celia, who had been desultorily picking out a one-handed tune on the piano, jumped up in nervous surprise as Tom burst in on her.

The childish blond locks had fallen haphazardly over his furrowed brow, and he was obviously in a state of distress. "Celia! I must talk to you."

"Tom," she exclaimed, restraining with an effort the urge to throw herself into his outstretched arms.

"Oh, Celia," he choked. "I've been such a fool."

Her eyes glowed with a promise of comfort, but she withheld instant sympathy and forgiveness, remembering how hurtful Tom had been to her only two days before. "What happened, Tom?"

He shook his head in despair. "You were right about Barclay. I'm finished with him. But please tell me it's not too late. I love you," he implored.

Celia's face lit with joy, and she stretched out her hands. Instantly Tom fell into her arms and buried his golden head in the soft curve of her shoulder. His remorseful endearments, murmured into his beloved's receptive ear, were the last words Regina heard as she quietly slipped from her seat in the corner and closed the door of the room behind her.

Hurrying down the hall to her uncle's study, she knocked once, then charged in impulsively. "Uncle Arthur," she cried with uncharacteristic excitement. "It's happened. Everything is going to be all right."

"Yes, Regina?" Arthur Cressley said mildly, looking up from his books. "What is it?"

"Tom and Celia have made it up. He's in there now." Regina smiled happily.

"That's nice," the vicar said in his usual restrained way. "I hope you are not too disappointed, my dear." And he turned back to his desk.

Regina felt a stab of compunction. Even her imperceptive uncle expected her to be dashed at the news. Apparently no one would believe that she was enormously pleased and relieved at the turn of events, even if she had to admit it was no thanks to her. The vicar had removed his glasses and was leaning on his folded hands. Regina sighed and dropped a kiss on the top of his gray head before tiptoeing away. He had never reproached her for her role in the broken engagement, but this comment suggested that he had felt a certain resentment.

Celia and Tom spent a long time together, and when they came out, it was to tell Regina and Mr. Cressley that they wanted him to marry them in the church exactly as they had planned. Moments later they roared away in the motor car to share their happiness with the Dawlishes at the Grange.

Regina watched them go with a mixture of emotions. The day had been a long one for her. The church service had seemed interminable, and the hymns, collection, and sermon had faded in and out of her consciousness with disconcerting irregularity. She had even found herself standing alone when everyone else had sunk back to their seats in a rustle of petticoats and prayer-book pages.

Regina had been thinking over, almost reliving, every moment of her shattering encounter with Alistair.

He had been hard on her, she thought self-defensively. If she had been mistaken in believing that he was infatuated with Miss Farnsworth, Regina could hardly be blamed. His behavior might have fooled anyone. As for the fact that Alistair condemned her for putting business before her personal life, it simply showed how biased his point of view was. Didn't he realize how difficult it had been for her with everyone expecting her to fail? And when she didn't, her success was discounted because she was sure to marry and toss aside the business at any moment. Regina had taught herself to be disciplined, controlled, to think before she acted, but she was far from the selfish, care-for-nobody Alistair believed her to be. She burned for a chance to prove to him how very wrong he was.

At dinner her relatives found her unusually silent, and when she left the chicken untasted on her plate, even Uncle Arthur noticed.

"Are you well, Regina?" he asked kindly, peering at her nearsightedly.

"Oh, yes."

But even with that prompting, she found it difficult to attend to the conversation. The thought of leaving Grantly without making peace with Alistair was troubling. If they parted on this note, she'd never see him again, a conclusion far from her desires.

Only after Celia and Tom's happy departure for the Grange did Regina's fertile brain devise a truly daring solution to her problem. Inevitably, she had been influenced by Tom's surprising *volte-face*. It seemed a happy omen, for if those two children could resolve their quarrel, she and Alistair should have no difficulty in following suit.

These weeks in Grantly had aroused dormant and unexplored passions in the hitherto sober-minded Miss Cressley. Now they burst forth, inspiring a plan that enchanted Regina with its brilliant simplicity. Though she did not want the confining and conventional role of wife and mother, why should she deny herself or Alistair the joy and tenderness of love itself? How unfair it would be, Regina thought rebelliously, to miss life's ultimate experience because of an outdated notion of propriety. After all, they were both free, and no one need know, save themselves. She would prove to him that she had a wealth of tenderness stored away in her heart, as much as any other woman. Regina knew she would make an execrable wife, but she rather fancied herself in the role of lover. Alistair wanted her; he had made that clear. And her own tempestuous reaction to him proved that she returned his ardor. If the timid Mrs. Dawlish had found the courage for such a step, why not the indomitable Miss Cressley?

Taking comfort from this unlikely example, Regina's only other worry was that her quarrel with Alistair might have given him a hearty disgust of her. Perhaps he had even ceased to care. But then, she dismissed that fear as absurd. He was angry, no doubt, but that was far from indifference.

Fired with enthusiasm for her newfound scheme, Regina decided on immediate action. Once in his presence, she was convinced that she could show Alistair just how supremely happy they both could be with this arrangement. Of course, the situation called for discretion and a modicum of guile; Regina had no desire to appear too forward. But no tears, she vowed, and no missish attempts to flirt. She would be reasonable, calm, and ultimately persuasive.

The telegram arrived just as Regina was about to don her most sensible hat and walk to the priory. She answered the door herself and accepted the yellow envelope. In no mood to be faced with any other urgency when there was but one overriding thought in her mind, she read the message at a glance.

LASSITER'S SHARES BOUGHT BY UNKNOWN THIRD
STOP COME BACK AT ONCE STOP CHIN UP STOP
HODGEKISS

Regina's initial reaction was annoyance, mingled with relief. At least Thwait and Pucey had not been the victors. Then worry edged in. Was the buyer simply another string to the colonel's bow? Unlikely, she felt. But whoever it was, she would convince, woo, and win him as she had done others in the past. Even if she was ousted, it would be but a temporary defeat, she told herself stoutly. It undoubtedly meant another battle similar to those she had fought in the past. But this time around, she felt weary at the mere prospect.

It would be wonderful to talk it over with Alistair, she thought in a sudden rush of optimism. He, of all people, understood what it meant to her and had the business sense that made his reactions worth having. With that opening, she at least had a foot in the door if all else failed.

Pinning her hat firmly in place, she walked over to the priory in the afternoon sunlight, her appearance as precise and businesslike as always. The only clue to her corked-down feelings were the two spots of color that burned in her cheeks. The momentum of decision carried her until she was admitted by the butler and bidden to wait in a gloomy chamber lined with leather-bound tomes. This was clearly where her uncle composed his scholarly and sleep-inducing sermons.

It was only moments later that Lord Grantham opened the door and stood staring at her, but they were crucial moments. She had had time to regret this impetuous rush to see a man who had shown the greatest dislike of her at their last meeting. If she had thrown herself into his arms, things might have taken a very different turn. As it was, she maintained a careful dignity.

"Well, Regina. This is a surprise," Alistair said matter-of-factly.

His face was hard to read, but what was visible was not reassuring.

"I came . . ." she began, then stopped and cleared her throat. "I came to say that I'm sorry if I offended you yesterday. You were right when you accused me of leaping to conclusions. Wrong conclusions, evidently."

"You believe me, then, when I say that I have no interest, except kindness, in Miss Farnsworth."

"Yes," she acknowledged. "But I do think my mistake was natural."

"Regina, what do you want?" Alistair asked softly, closing the massive library door behind him.

"Just for us not to part as we did yesterday," she said with an effort. "I am not so unfeeling as you think."

A wave of uncertainty shook her resolve, and she wondered for a frantic moment what she was doing there. Alistair was distant, polite, as if she were a perfect stranger. But then, she reasoned, his pique had yet to be cajoled away. The Earl of Grantham would not forgive so easily. "Can't we be friends again?" Regina smiled.

"What sort of friendship are you suggesting?" he asked skeptically.

Alistair was making this very hard for her, Regina thought with a flash of resentment. "You hinted at a deeper relationship, and at the time I was not interested. Since then I've changed my mind."

The earl strolled over to her and with an expression of quizzical amusement on his face looked Regina up and down as if he were considering buying a prize heifer. "An interesting offer," he drawled. "I take it you are proposing to me."

Nettled and slightly deflated by that less than chivalrous answer, Regina was quick to correct his mistaken impression. "I am proposing nothing. It was you who offered. I am accepting."

Even Regina could not help but know that this was not the way these arrangements were usually conducted. She had come as close as she dared to complete surrender; the rest was up to Alistair. Shouldn't he be kissing the hem of her gown or some other absurdity?

Instead he was regarding her with extreme wariness. *That's what comes of taking the initiative,* Regina glowered to herself. *Even the most ardent lover backs off in fear.*

"I'm overcome by your candor, Regina. But I'm at a loss to account for your sudden change of heart."

"I'm not sure either," was her miffed response. She crossed to the large French window that led to the south side of the terrace. "I suppose it was seeing Tom and Celia make up that prompted me to discover if we could do the same."

"So the lovers are together again."

"And don't tell me not to be too unhappy about

it," she flashed over her shoulder. "Uncle thinks I'm ready to throw myself into the nearest ditch."

"I give you more credit than that," he smiled. "And I heartily applaud your logic in deciding that if two green children have sense enough to tie the knot, the state of matrimony cannot be too dreadful after all."

Regina's back was to him so she did not see Lord Grantham taking the inevitable step toward her that would have ended in the breathless declaration of love she so eagerly awaited. Her words stopped him cold.

"Of course, marriage has no place in our plans. They are young enough to adjust to each other. You and I require a more flexible situation."

"Flexible?" he inquired in a strange tone.

"Certainly. I doubt if I could escape from Manchester more than twice a month. And once Parliament is in session again, even you will find it difficult to get away. We should buy a small cottage somewhere in the Midlands so neither of us has to travel too far." Her practical mind was already on the details that an arrangement like theirs entailed.

"What about our families?" Alistair asked in a dangerously smooth voice.

Regina was nothing if not pragmatic. "They need never find out if we are discreet. Surely you've been successful at conducting your affairs in private before this. Besides, it's no one's business but our own."

"Forgive me if I seem a bit obtuse, but before

you begin purchasing furniture for our love nest, may I enquire if our liaison is to be illicit?"

Regina flushed. "Alistair, there's no need to be crude."

"Why not? What you are suggesting is vulgar in the extreme. Even if I agreed to your scheme, isn't it the man's duty to procure the trysting place? Of course, you would expect me to bestow a few favors on you, I hope. Some diamond earrings perhaps, and a lap dog for consolation on the nights I find myself too busy to come to you. They tell me it's the pecuniary benefits that make this kind of relationship so inviting. And in return I get the exclusive rights to your lily-pure body."

"Why are you making it sound so sordid?" Regina protested. "We could be very happy."

Lord Grantham's raking gaze looked very much like anger, and Regina cast around in her mind for a more persuasive argument. She fumbled with her reticule and closed her fingers over the crumpled telegram she had hastily stuffed inside. Perhaps this would help her explain that she wanted more from him than a few snatched hours of physical bliss. A union of the mind as well as the body. That was not so reprehensible, and he could keep his precious diamonds. She held out the paper in mute appeal.

"What's this?" He read it swiftly, then tossed it back at her. "So! You think you've lost your business. How sad, Regina." Breathing hard, he controlled himself with an effort. "It certainly explains why you suddenly appeared on my doorstep. I suppose that since you've lost the most important thing in your life, as you describe it, it might not be too painful if you could console yourself with me. I should be flattered that you think so highly of my skills as a lover, though I doubt you'll need them but temporarily. Don't worry, Regina, you are quite resilient. There's no need to sacrifice your scruples to this degree. In a few weeks, when you've had time to gather your resources, you'll be champing at the bit, ready to fight and win back your indisputable sovereignty."

This was not going the way Regina had planned at all. Instead of rejoicing at her capitulation, Alistair was angry about it. Surely he couldn't have thought she meant marriage by her blushing acceptance of his offer. But he did, she realized with a start. "Alistair, you don't understand. My reference to Tom and Celia had nothing to do with our situation."

"Obviously."

"I meant only that two people who care for each other can resolve their differences."

"So you think you can resolve love by dishonor."

For an instant Regina wished she were the kind of woman who could summon up tears at will, because if she gave in to her inclinations, she'd smash the Earl of Grantham over the head with one of those weighty tomes on the shelf. And at all costs she must remain calm and reasonable. "Now it is you who is being illogical. Who made speeches about the joys of togetherness? Not I. But I do admit that your arguments are valid. There is no sense in forgoing all pleasures in life; why not have the best of both worlds?"

"It is interesting that you came to this conclusion only this afternoon. That telegram has nothing to do with it, of course."

"Alistair, that is not why I'm here," she protested. "It's not even important to us." Regina knew her denial was falling on deaf ears, but she couldn't bring herself to beg. If he loved or wanted her at all, he'd take her on any terms, she reasoned. How much more must she humble herself?

The earl took a step back and bowed ironically. "Forgive me, but I fear I must decline so generous an offer. Not that it doesn't have a certain appeal, but I am not in the market for an affair at this time. If you were to peddle your wares at a future date, I might be in a more receptive frame of mind. But right now I find the idea both distasteful and personally insulting."

Regina was rigid with shock. This callous rejection was the last thing she expected. To feel so cheapened, so humiliated, by an honest show of love. But was it honest? Regina could hardly think straight. She had offered this man her heart and soul, and he refused it. Yet in all fairness, she had to admit that her presentation lacked a certain finesse. In fact, she showed all the delicacy and tenderness of a combatant in a boardroom brawl. And this was one time she wanted everything to go right. Apparently logic was not the proper appeal when one is bent on seduction. She might have done better submitting her request by registered mail. *I'm out of my element,* Regina thought in bitter reflection. *And Alistair has left me to flounder in this quicksand alone.*

The only thing left was to salvage whatever pride still remained to her after this debacle.

Regina gave a semblance of a scornful laugh. "What a stuffed shirt you are, Alistair. I had hoped for better from you. There is nothing shameful in an adult relationship. You seemed in favor of it yourself at one time."

"Not with a woman of your class."

"Class be damned! I'm no different from any of your doxies; and I'm sure you've had a string of them. Let it be a lesson to you, Lord Grantham: Women are all the same. We're greedy, grasping little things, with no more morality to our nature than a bitch in heat. There! You see how vulgar I can be? A lucky escape for you. But now that I've discovered this unsuspected but infinitely interesting aspect of my character, I realize that you are much too tame for me. I thank you for my initial education, but now it's on to bigger and better things. I might even work my way through every man on the board."

"Regina! Stop it!"

She drew herself up with dignity. "I'm sorry if I misunderstood your intentions, Lord Grantham. It was not my purpose to insult you in any way. Please forgive my intrusion. You will not see me again."

Blindly she walked out of the room.

CHAPTER TWELVE

When the train pulled into Bath it was nearly dinner time, but food was far from Regina's thoughts. Although changing her destination had been a matter of impulse, she could not claim to be acting on instinct. Even as a child, Regina had rarely run to her mother for comfort. And it was not maternal solicitude that she craved now, so much as the answer to some troubling questions. Of course, chances were her mother would be of little help; yet Regina was there. She might as well try.

A porter quickly transferred her luggage to a waiting cab that drove her from the congested city center to a distant neighborhood of semidetached cottages, each with its pocket-handkerchief garden in front. It was all rawly new, and the saplings that adorned most doorways had all the height of a good-sized man.

Regina stared in amazement as the cab pulled up in front of what was clearly the newest house of all, its miniature lawn still more bare earth than spindly grass.

"Here ye be, miss. Number four, Rose Trellis Lane."

The address was correct, but Regina told the cabbie to wait. It was hard to believe that her mother had chosen to move to this middle-class environment. Mrs. Cressley had written that she had given up the lease on her townhouse in a fashionable section of Bath to purchase her own place in the suburbs, but Regina had never imagined that it would look like this. What was the attraction of these dreary little homes, each exactly like the other? Regina knocked on the door, half expecting to be told there was some mistake and that Mrs. Cressley was unknown here. But the maid who opened the door was recognizably her mother's.

"Miss Regina," she gasped. "We didn't expect you."

"Hello, Agnes. How are you? I thought I'd surprise Mother."

"She'll be surprised, doubtless," Agnes said a touch grimly.

Regina smiled. Agnes had always been on the sour side. Paying off the cabbie and overseeing the removal of the cases, which were dumped unceremoniously in the tiny entry hall, was the work of a moment. But when Agnes told Regina to wait in the sitting room and her mother still did not appear, Regina was a bit put out. The cramped area was filled to overflowing with well-remembered pieces brought from the Manchester house five years before, but their rather heavy magnificence seemed incongruous in this modest chamber. The sideboard reached within inches of the low ceiling, she noted critically.

Impatiently Regina looked out the door and

down the hall, where a green baize door swung open briefly and as quickly shut again. The kitchen staff peering out to check on the guest's appearance, Regina surmised hazily. But where was her mother? Was she to be kept waiting indefinitely? Before Regina could summon up the energy to go in search of her missing parent, a smiling woman appeared in the doorway.

"Regina, dear. Why didn't you warn me you were coming?" The portly figure enveloped her daughter in a warm hug, her gray-brown hair in disarray and her cheeks flushed from exertion. Still, her smile was warmly welcoming, though she seemed slightly out of breath.

"Mother, you sound almost guilty. Not hiding a man in the linen cupboard, are you?" Regina was the only one to laugh at the sally, but it passed unnoticed as she felt a rush of pleasure in seeing her mother again. They had never been particularly close, although there was great affection on both sides. She regarded her mother now with fond eyes. "Why, you look marvelous. A bit more weight, but you are positively glowing. But why the move? Did living in town become too noisy? You should have warned me that you had turned into a middle-class householder. I can't imagine why, but it suits you."

Mrs. Cressley laughed uncomfortably and flushed even more. Then she made her own inspection. "Ginny, dear, you look exhausted. Have you been overworking again? Oh, I am glad to see you, darling. There's something I need to talk to you about. But it can wait. What brings you here so suddenly? Is it a business trip?" Noticing the two large cases for the first time, she asked doubtfully, "Are you staying here?"

Regina thought her mother seemed unusually nervous. "Just for the night. I'm on the way home from Surrey. Uncle Arthur and Celia send their love."

"How are they?" Mrs. Cressley asked vaguely. "But isn't changing at Bath rather the long way home?"

"I need to talk to you. A letter might have done as well, but . . . we haven't been together in so long," she finished lamely.

"Darling, what a sweet girl you are. I've missed you too. Sit right here, and I'll have Agnes take your bags upstairs. Tea is on; you know I never eat heavily in the evening, just a light repast, then you can go to bed. Are you hungry?"

"But our talk?"

"Oh, yes . . . well, as soon as I . . . I see that our supper is being prepared."

"Good, I'll come with you. I'd love to see the rest of the house."

"No! I mean, it's so untidy right now. Just wait right here, and I'll bring our food."

"Don't you have a dining room?"

Virginia Cressley looked scandalized. "Of course. This house has every modern amenity, including a separate scullery. It might seem small to you after that drafty mansion in Manchester, but it is exactly the right size for me and . . . Agnes."

"I'm not criticizing, only curious why we must eat in the sitting room. There's no table here. You don't expect me to balance a plate on my lap, do you? Honestly, Mother, you needn't treat me like company. I'd be glad to eat in the kitchen, if you'd prefer."

"I'm afraid that's impossible. The man . . . the cabinetmaker is in there, and you know what a mess they work in; all that lumber and . . . and hammers. Yes, that's what it is, hammers."

"At this time of night?" Regina asked. "Never mind. Skip the kitchen."

Virginia Cressley expelled a sigh of relief when Regina sat back down on the sofa without demurring further. She fully expected her daughter to insist on a full-scale inspection of the house to make sure her mother hadn't squandered her money on a poor investment. But, happily, Regina seemed uninterested in the details, and Mrs. Cressley hurried off to see about a meal for them.

Regina was only marginally aware of her mother's odd behavior. Normally Mrs. Cressley was far more effusive at a rare visit from her daughter. But perhaps she was worried that Regina would not approve of this peculiar move of hers. Not that it mattered. Virginia was certainly free to do exactly as she liked, even if it meant living in middle-class obscurity in the suburbs of Bath. This modest dwelling was far from the sort of home she had always known. She had even dismissed some of her domestic staff, it seemed. But of course, in this doll's house there would scarcely be place for all of them.

Her mother returned and ushered her across the hall into a tiny room, where she was seated at a small, round table. "The carpenter has left, so we can be quite cozy."

"But what have you done with the dining room furniture?" Regina's glance fell on the single hutch against the wall.

"I've put a great deal of furniture in storage. All that mahogany was simply superfluous here. Would you like it back? Here, darling, try this ham roll. I made it only this morning."

"You made it! How strange. What happened to Alfred? I didn't even know you could cook!"

"I'm learning and having a wonderful time. It's a . . . hobby. As for Alfred, he received a truly munificent offer from Lady Pinkham, and I encouraged him to take it. I didn't need a French chef, the little entertaining I do."

"Mmmm. This is delicious." Regina was tucking into the meal with an appetite that was natural under the circumstances. It was the first food she had been able to stomach in over twenty-four hours. "But you do have a cook, don't you? I don't approve of you working in the kitchen."

"Oh, yes. Mrs. Bangors. An estimable woman. But I enjoy cooking now and then for Ber . . . I mean, it's something interesting to do."

Regina accepted this stumbling explanation at face value. The fact was, she was not listening too attentively. Instead she was busy wondering how to ask her mother questions they had never discussed before.

The meal finished, her mother was anxious to return to the parlor again. So Agnes could clean up, she apologized.

"Poor Agnes does the clearing up?" Regina marveled. "I'm amazed she would condescend to do such a mundane chore. In the old days I think she limited her efforts to brushing your hair and laying out dresses for you to choose."

"Agnes and I have been together so long that we understand one another. Moving a few dishes to the kitchen is not such a terrible job. I even do it myself now and then."

"You shouldn't be doing housework, Mother. Do you need an increase in your allowance? We can run to fifty maids, you know."

"That's silly. I need some occupation, after all. And this tiny house is so simple to keep up."

"Are you bored . . . or lonely?" Regina asked, suddenly conscience-stricken that she had never considered this before.

"Of course not, you foolish girl. My bridge club meets every Thursday, and on Saturday afternoons there is an open-air concert in the park. I don't lack for friends either, you know."

"I'm glad to hear it," Regina said awkwardly. She was becoming acutely aware that this pleasant woman seated near her was a virtual stranger. She knew very little of her life, had always simply taken her for granted. Guilt made

Regina doubtful how to ask the questions she had come to pose. Perhaps Alistair had been right about her all along; she had shut out the people who loved her.

"Mother, I . . ."

"Regina, dear . . ."

Both stopped at once. Mrs. Cressley cleared her throat to begin again, but then noticed Regina twisting her hands together nervously. This was so unlike the coolly controlled young woman she knew, that she realized this was no ordinary visit. In the regular course of events Regina would be poring over her mother's accounts and suggesting improvements in her household arrangements. That she showed no interest in this was cause for alarm. Motherlike, Mrs. Cressley forgot about her own particular revelation in concern for her daughter.

"Is something wrong, dear?" Her pleasant face creased in worry. This reticence was unlike Regina's usual forthright manner. The situation must be dire indeed. Perhaps she had had a serious business reversal.

"Were you happy with Father?" Regina blurted out.

Mrs. Cressley was understandably taken aback. "What an odd question."

"That was terribly impertinent. Forgive me." Regina crossed to the window and looked out at the empty street, illuminated by a single gas lamp. "Was Father a tyrant?" She couldn't resist asking.

"Whatever gave you that idea? He was a very considerate gentleman."

"But he did bully you."

"I swear, Regina, I don't know how you came to such a silly notion. He was a fine husband. A bit stubborn at times, but all men are like that."

"Oh, Mother! Did you never want to be free? Don't look so scandalized. I didn't mean divorce."

"I should hope not. I loved your father dearly, so why should I have wanted to be free of him? The subject of emancipation has taken too much hold on you, dear. Penelope's doing, no doubt."

"I thought you admired her."

"I do. Immensely. But she frightens me to death with all her talk of votes and women's rights. I'm not sure I approve. Your father was quite adamant about it."

"That is precisely what I mean," Regina charged. "He despised any form of independence for women. He gave you an allowance, then made you accountable to him for every penny you spent."

"You give me an allowance too," Mrs. Cressley argued with great logic, "and that doesn't appear to disturb you."

"But it's from the business."

"So? Where do you think your father got his wherewithal? Regina, you make no sense. Are you suggesting that I was entitled to unlimited credit? Where would the stock exchange be if everyone demanded extravagant dividends? I thought you were such a brilliant businesswoman."

"But you never had a say in how your money was invested, while he insisted that you account for every minor expenditure."

"Regina," her mother said firmly, "I have a poor head when it comes to money, and it was your father's place to take care of me. I expected that from him."

"How could you be so humble?"

"Because I am not you, dear. I wanted to be taken care of. Your father understood and approved."

Regina understood too. Rather than a victim, her mother was a willing participant in the game of master and follower. Only did it have to be that way? Alistair promised not. But he was still a man, wasn't he? He would naturally want to reign supreme.

"Mother, please understand that I'm not prying, but didn't you ever feel that you had made a mistake? That perhaps without Father, you might have done what you wanted, been free to indulge yourself, travel perhaps? I can't believe you were content to sit back and let him run your life for you."

Virginia Cressley regarded her daughter with loving exasperation. How silly the child was. She had yet to learn that all solutions don't come in neat little packages. For a modern woman, she was very unenlightened. How like Walter she was at times, so afraid to be at a disadvantage. If she ever made a false move, there'd be no living with her outraged remorse. Neither father nor daughter liked to feel they had been unfair, but both reserved that bit of private territory on which no one could trespass. In turn they did everything they could for the other person's good, never realizing that such confining kindness created a barrier. What they construed as help was, in reality, benevolent despotism. For Mrs. Cressley it was a comfortable state of affairs, but Regina, more like her father than she realized, chafed at such restrictions.

Mrs. Cressley was afraid that making her daughter understand this was beyond her modest capabilities, yet she tried. "Ginny, darling, don't equate my situation with your own. You know what a helpless creature I am, not at all brave like you. It was a relief to me that your father could handle my affairs so efficiently. I despised the idea of talking to bankers and lawyers. As for the personal side of our marriage, Walter was an ideal husband. Even you must have realized how he cherished me."

"Smothered you."

"No, dear. For me it was security. My requirements are not yours. You are too much like your father to appreciate coddling. Whenever I wanted him to do something against his own judgment, I was forced to use guile. But you see, it was really no more reprehensible than his making certain decisions for me. None of us are very wise when it comes to our own good; sometimes it takes someone else to see what is best. Walter would never admit to a cold, so I had to pretend I had one before he would call for a doctor. Then, of course, we could claim that the prescribed medicine was only a preventative, in case he caught it from me. Silly shams, but accommodating on both sides. He catered to my foibles, and I returned the favor."

"Does it always have to be that way?" Regina asked dispiritedly.

"Of course not. But I could never have been happy under other circumstances."

Mrs. Cressley's smile of placid sweetness was Regina's undoing. How could she have imagined her mother to be repining all those years? Virginia Cressley was a picture of contentment. Regina had conveniently twisted the obvious so it was colored with subversive overtones. Walter Cressley was as much a victim of his wife's expectations as she was of his dominance. He might have been a different sort of husband if he'd had a less dependent wife. But it didn't matter really; they suited each other.

Then Regina did something she hadn't done in years. She burst into tears and threw herself into her mother's arms. "Oh, Mama, I'm so miserable."

Mrs. Cressley was unprepared for the role of comforter, as Regina had always been an independent child who scorned any fuss being made over her. Now she was given a chance to do what she had always dreamed of, and she held her daughter lovingly. "Oh, my dearest, what is it?" Her arms enfolded Regina, and there was a look of utter bliss on her face.

Regina sobbed uncontrollably for a few minutes

before withdrawing from the comfortable haven of her mother's embrace. "This is all so silly," she choked, stemming the heavy flow of tears to an occasional trickle. "I don't know what came over me."

But Mrs. Cressley, with age-old maternal clairvoyance, understood very well, and her eyes glowed with delight. "Who is he?"

Regina cast her mother a look of awestruck wonder. "How did you know?"

"My darling girl, when a woman who prides herself on absolute control of her life suddenly questions every tenet of her convictions . . . and comes running to her foolish little mother, then she must have come a real cropper."

Regina had to smile at that cant expression coming from the fashionable Mrs. Cressley. "Isn't it ridiculous for a woman of my age to behave so . . . so. . . . I think I've lost my senses altogether."

"Love is not rational, but delightful, nonetheless."

"Do I seem delighted?"

"It was bound to come as a shock to you since you were so unprepared. But, Regina, I hope you are not jeopardizing your happiness because of some foolish ideas about your father and me."

"It seems I was harboring a lot of misconceptions, but I've always prided myself on remaining detached from this sort of illusory emotion. It blinds you to reality, and above all, I hope I'm realistic. A husband has no place in my life. There isn't room for one."

"Then why are you crying?"

Regina had no satisfactory answer for that. Why was she crying? "He said I wouldn't be expected to give up my career, but I don't believe him."

"Then you don't love him enough. A husband does deserve your trust at the very least, but if you can't give him that, then your affections cannot be very deeply engaged."

Regina considered that for a moment. "I love him with all my heart . . . but I'm still frightened."

"It's always disconcerting to stand on the brink without taking that first step. But you must believe that he'll catch you if you fall. Just go back and tell him you've reconsidered. That is not capitulation, Regina, but acceptance."

Regina had regained her composure, but she looked at her mother in dumb defeat. "It doesn't matter. I muffed it. He doesn't want me anymore."

"Oh, my dear," Mrs. Cressley exclaimed in sympathetic tones. "But perhaps there is still a chance. His pride may be hurt, to be sure, but a touch of flattery could put things right. All men need to feel the tiniest bit superior."

"He's not like that."

"Then he must be a paragon indeed. Come, Regina, moping isn't going to solve anything. I'll fix us a nice cup of tea, and we'll plan our strategy."

Mrs. Cressley was in her element. Not only did she have a daughter to comfort, but bringing around recalcitrant males was her specialty. Having had many years' practice on an extremely stubborn husband, one bruised swain posed no particular problem. It was her intractable daughter who required judicious handling.

But before she could even rise from her chair, a monumental uproar issued from the back of the house. This time there was no thought of keeping Regina from rushing pell-mell into the kitchen. Mrs. Cressley hardly spared a thought to what her daughter might discover, as her own terror was uppermost. They reached the tiny kitchen to find a scene of great confusion. Agnes was on her knees, hovering over what seemed to be a great deal of broken crockery. Above her, waving a hammer about lethally, was a fearsome-looking man in baggy pants and shirt-sleeves. The carpenter, no doubt.

"I warned you not to put those things back on the shelf until I fixed the support. You stupid girl, your mistress will be sick when she sees this mess."

"Bernard!" Mrs. Cressley shrieked. "What happened?"

The man regarded her in abject guilt, which immediately turned to fury at the glowering Agnes. "That confounded idiot replaced all the dishes, and I hadn't repaired the shelf yet. All this furtive sneaking around has cost you, madam."

"How was I to know he hadn't fixed it, ma'am? He's been at it long enough." Agnes stared accusingly at the carpenter.

Bernard gave Mrs. Cressley a telling glance. "Well? Have you told her yet?" He inclined his massive head toward Regina.

There was a moment of breathless silence in the room, then Mrs. Cressley met her daughter's eyes in embarrassment. "This isn't how I meant to break the news to you, but you might as well know now." She stepped quietly over to Bernard and, with great dignity, presented him. "Regina, this is Bernard Cavendish . . . my husband. Your new father."

There was an expression of tremulous pride on her face that begged for approval, but Regina was dumbstruck at the sight of her mother clinging to the stalwart arm of this enormous stranger. He was like her late father in build and coloring, but his steel-gray eyes flashed ominously at her from under a pair of thick, uncompromising brows.

Before today's revelations Regina would have been horrified at her mother's choosing such a one to succeed Walter Cressley. Now she knew better, though she would have thought her mother could look higher than a common laborer. But the fact that they had married secretly, hiding away in this obscure suburb, humbled Regina to her knees. Was she such a tyrant, an autocrat, that her own mother lived in dread of her wrath? It

was a sobering thought, but one she faced un-
flinchingly. It appeared that all the things she
despised about her father were her own worst
faults, and perhaps, not his at all. Walter Cressley,
with all his autocratic ways, had not inspired
terror, but his daughter, it seemed, had become
absolutely intimidating.

Yet not everything about her was so reprehensible. Blind and obdurate, to be sure, but with it,
she had only wanted what was best for her
mother. That in itself wasn't selfish, but who had
given Regina Cressley the right to dictate the
terms? Just as she nearly succeeded in ruining
Celia's life, she might have done the same to her
mother. How arrogant to judge without the least
perception. Alistair was right; she did set herself
up as judge and executioner. At least she wasn't a
snob. This carpenter had a certain magnificence
that she couldn't help but admire.

Bernard Cavendish had not taken his gaze off
the woman who could assuage his wife's anxiety,
and Regina recognized his defensive attitude.
Here was an ideal mate for a wife who wanted to
be cosseted and protected, and from the look of
him, Bernard Cavendish was ready to do just
that. How humiliating for a man of his stamp to
hide in the kitchen, waiting to be summoned out
for inspection. It would be mortifying if it weren't
so funny. One lone female, deficient and indefen-
sible herself, must relieve these two people of
their unnecessary apprehensions.

All eyes were on Regina.

"What can I say? I'm surprised, of course, but absolutely delighted. Can I kiss my new father?"

Virginia Cavendish let out a cry of delight and flung herself into her daughter's open arms. Bernard Cavendish then followed suit, though his embrace was less exuberant.

"I told your mother she was getting in a stew over nothing. Any daughter of hers had to be just as sweet and loving." The newlyweds exchanged a look of warm affection that included Regina. "So what say we put up that pot of tea, though we might be drinking out of saucers, and then I'll show you the rest of the house. I know you think it odd that your mother would move to such an outlandish address, but I'm a builder, my girl, and this whole area is Cavendish Estates, a high-powered name for these little boxes, but that's why we're here. If the builder himself won't live in them, who will? But it's not for long. As soon as we've sold the last one, your mother and I are taking a long cruise."

"So you are 'Canny Cavendish,'" Regina said with respect. "I should have recognized your name. They say you revolutionized the house-building industry with your ability to keep prices down. It's all done by duplication, I see. Very clever, indeed. The shells are the same, but the insides can be anything the housewife wants."

Bernard took her hand in his great fist. "It's going to be interesting having a businesswoman as a daughter. Mind you don't put me to the blush. I haven't your knack for adding in the millions.

You're a mite famous yourself. A wizard, they say."

"I could use a bit of sorcery right now," Regina said wryly.

"Never you mind. They don't call me canny for nothing." He shepherded both ladies out of the kitchen and back into the sitting room, with an order for Agnes to put up a pot. "Now, I couldn't help overhearing some of your talk. So sit you down and tell me all about it. We'll get you your fellow back quicker than a splinter in a thumb."

Regina had to laugh at his blunt words, though her spirits were still at a low ebb. Still, he was her father, wasn't he, and for that dubious honor, deserved her trust. At least she was taking a step in the right direction. He was the first man on whom she had conferred that tribute in years. The other who merited that same reliance probably no longer cared. The tears welled up again.

"I appreciate your concern," she sniffed, "but I'm afraid it's too late."

CHAPTER THIRTEEN

For two weeks Manchester had been sweltering in a heat wave that slowed production and shortened tempers. Gentlemen were appearing in the streets bareheaded and in shirt-sleeves, while ladies of lesser quality exposed an indecent amount of neck and shoulder. Urchins played in the gutters as harried firemen on their way to yet another minor disaster squirted the little perishers with great gusts from the heavy hoses to shoo them away. The children reveled in the cool water that splashed over their hot, dirty feet and followed the red wagons, shouting curses and obscenities that might warrant yet another blast of water from the irate firemen.

From the fourth floor of Cressley Limited, Regina watched the activity below with apathy, not even smiling when a well-dressed gentleman became the accidental target of the fire brigade and opened his umbrella to ward off the small shower. Nothing had held any interest for her since her return from Bath, and she wondered dully if the next hour would finally quell the last vestiges of her spirit. It was unlike her to fall into such a depression, but never before had she doubted her own wisdom, and with such good cause.

Dottie poked an inquisitive head through the

doorway of the office. "Aren't you ready yet? The directors are waiting."

"Does anyone rush to his own execution, Dottie? At least allow me the luxury of a last cigarette."

"Miss Cressley, you are being unduly morbid. There is no reason to suppose that this new man will make any appreciable difference to your position. Besides, didn't John promise that you would be pleased with his decision? If that is no comfort, what about the fight that may await you? You've always relished one before."

Regina appreciated Dottie's attempt to buck up her spirits, but she replied with a wry twist of her lips, "The moment cannot be put off any longer it seems. My sword, please."

Her efficient secretary handed over the bulky stack of ledger books and followed her employer down the dark-paneled hallway to the conference room. Regina paused before entering, almost overcome with dread, but immediately she assumed her coolest expression and walked in briskly.

The conference room had been designed by Walter Cressley to give him a psychological advantage at these board meetings, and successive managing directors had profited by the arrangement. A long oak table lined by uncushioned, high-backed chairs on either side was headed by a small dais on which rested a seat of such magnificent proportions that it resembled a throne. It was fashioned of black oak, ornately carved into the semblance of a writhing dragon, its arms, taloned claws, the head mounted high over brown velvet cushions. Regina could not fill the chair physically, for its dimensions were suited to some Viking king, but from its eminence she had dominated affairs at Cressley Limited for eight years. The spot directly across from her at the opposite end of the table was, by long custom, left vacant. The directors were arranged on either side, because it was felt by Walter Cressley that someone facing the managing director might seem to rival him.

Regina took her place and scanned the familiar faces, looking for the new man, but he hadn't arrived as yet. Was he planning a grand entrance? John Lassiter's chair was certainly empty and waiting for him.

There was a sense of drama in the occasion of today's meeting. Rumor had it that it was to be the end of a reign, and all felt a certain trepidation at the possibility of change. They knew where they were with Miss Cressley, and few present wanted to tamper with success. With so much at stake, it was surprising that no one had managed to ferret out the identity of the new director. Even Colonel Pucey claimed ignorance, though some suspected, quite wrongly, that he knew more than he admitted. But John Lassiter had not divulged the name of the purchaser, no doubt as a last appeasing gesture of friendship to Regina. Although Pucey had every intention of winning the newcomer to his side, he felt as uneasy as everyone else as the silent wait stretched out. Then the door opened.

Regina kept her head down, pretending absorption in the papers before her, then heard a chair scrape across the floor. Slowly she lifted her eyes to feel them widen in shock as they halted on the figure seating himself at the foot of the table, where no one had ever dared sit before.

"Good afternoon, Miss Cressley. I'm sorry I'm late, but my cab was caught behind a fire wagon. Cumbersome things, but so necessary to our health and well-being. Gentlemen."

For a moment she couldn't get a word out, then in a shaky breath, "Gentlemen, may I present the Earl of Grantham."

"Please, don't let me delay things further," he smiled. "Go right ahead with your meeting. Since I'm a novice at these functions, just consider me an interested spectator today."

There was a murmur of surprise and recognition around the table before the men settled down to the business at hand. Frederick Pendennis read the minutes of the last meeting in his duty as secretary of the board of directors, followed by a lengthy biannual report from the treasurer. A few minor details were then dealt with, including the fittings for the new treadles and an up-to-date report on the impending strike of the dockworkers.

Regina conducted the meeting with only half a mind, as the rest of it was taken up with the astounding revelation that Alistair had somehow cut her out with John Lassiter. It was the basest, vilest of tricks. How could he have taken the very thing he knew she wanted so badly? How could any man sink so low, she asked herself in a rage. He had pretended friendship, even affection, while plotting so cruel a revenge. In comparison Lassiter's betrayal was merely a venial sin. It took all her courage, but Regina sat through the meeting, pretending a cool indifference to the morning's surprise. She could at least preserve her dignity.

The meeting rambled on as if its managing director had nothing better to do than listen to their babble, but, thankfully, there were no motions presented that might call for a vote or even a show of approval. Still, even without a major issue, the colonel was not above bringing things to a head and drawing the boundary lines that would force the earl to choose sides. But Pucey was in no particular hurry to challenge the status quo. There was groundwork to be done before engaging in combat, and he was too wily to rush his fences.

The formalities were concluded in just over an hour and when the meeting adjourned, the directors gathered around their new colleague and welcomed him to their ranks. A few were loud in their praises of Miss Cressley, but most chose to remain silent on that score, feeling a more conservative approach was called for until the situation clarified itself. Colonel Pucey was almost obsequious in his attempts to impress the earl, Regina noted with distaste, but Grantham displayed no particular aversion to his toadying manner. A man as important as Lord Grantham expected homage; it was his due. Yet Miss Cressley appeared disinclined to do a bit of politicking, and that, the colonel thought, was a card in his favor.

Regina hadn't moved from her seat and when the directors took their leave, followed by Miss Hodgekiss, she fully expected the earl to disappear out the door as well.

Instead he walked back to his seat and stood facing her down the long expanse of table, drawing out an envelope from his briefcase. "This is yours, I believe." Then, with a rather odd smile, he slid it down the highly polished table, and it came to a stop in front of Regina's fingers.

She flinched from the stark legal document until the earl's peremptory "Read it!" forced her to pick it up.

It was brief and to the point. The Earl of Grantham, owner of one hundred fifty thousand shares of stock in Cressley Limited, was relinquishing his prerogative to take his seat on the board of directors and, in keeping with the bylaws of the company, was duly turning over his voting proxy to the managing director, Regina Cressley. The earl would make no further claims from the stock, other than the dividends of ownership.

Regina's eyes flew to his. "I don't understand."

"It's simple. You are now the majority stockholder."

"I realize that. But why?"

"Why not? It's what you wanted, isn't it?"

That, of course, was no answer. The earl was making a staggering, unrealistic gesture. He had bought fifteen percent of Cressley Limited for an outlandish figure, and now, as if it were the most normal thing in the world, was giving away the power that came with it.

"If this is your way of cutting me down to size, a clean jab to the heart would have done as well."

"Ever the happy winner. That's what I like about you, Regina, you accept a gift with all the graciousness of a wounded eagle."

"Pardon me. Am I to thank you for my downfall?"

"Hear me out, if you please. I am not planning on overthrowing the managing director. My purpose is quite the opposite, in fact. I intend to insure your position."

Regina tossed the paper back on the table. "And what will I be expected to do? Lick your boots, give a public thank you whenever you happen to walk by?"

"You could start by trusting me. This is no trick. The business is now entirely controlled by Miss Regina Cressley. Of course, if you fall down on the job, the directors will try hard to replace you. They might not succeed, since you now have fifty-five percent of the voting stock. But no doubt you will simply go on to greater success. At any rate, I won't interfere. I'm sure you'll make a fortune for me. And remember, you hold the proxy; my hands are tied."

Regina regarded him warily. As he said, she did have voting control, so he couldn't possibly block her on that score. The question that remained was what he hoped to gain by it. Still, it was a fait accompli; why not take it? It gave her one advantage anyway. She got up from her chair and stepped down to the floor where mere earthlings walked. "I can't imagine why you are doing this, although I'm sure I'll soon find out, but in any case, I accept. The gift horse will bear examination at a later date."

"You still think I have an ulterior motive."

"Naturally. What else should I think?"

The earl tightened his lips. "You might try seeing it as an investment in you."

The retort died before it was uttered as Regina digested the meaning of his words. He was acknowledging her abilities as a businesswoman, and there was some balm in that. But Regina reminded herself that there is no such thing as a free lunch. She eyed him suspiciously; the man was as full of surprises as a fun house. A few moments ago she had tasted the bitterness of total defeat. Now fortune's wheel had spun again, and she held a victory of sorts in her hand, a victory whose price was yet to be determined. Still, the proxy was the culmination of twelve years of striving, and it could be withdrawn again by the man who faced her down the long table. It was time to be politic.

"I . . . I humbly thank you," Regina said,

sweeping him a low curtsy. "Your kindness overwhelms me, my lord."

"Confound it," he roared. "You can stop that groveling. Meekness does not suit you, especially as you'd like nothing better now than to stick a knife in my back. Damn, if a few shares of stock are going to turn you into a smarmy, toadying little miss, I'll take the bloody things back. Why don't you accuse me of coercion instead, blackmail, anything? Don't start kissing my hands."

"Take them back then," Regina charged. "If I want to be nice, I'll be nice. And I am not smarmy."

"That's better," he said approvingly. "You should always be yourself. Not that I object to a bit of sweetness, but never overdo a good thing."

Regina gazed at him in mounting irritation.

"Now," he said warmly. "Shall we begin again? I have no intention of interfering in your business life, Regina. Hence, the proxy. But I do intend to have a say in how we conduct ourselves out of the office."

"Then you do want to exercise some control," she charged.

"Not control," he contradicted. "I could have had that by not relinquishing the stock, but it would defeat my purpose."

His purpose. Suddenly she knew what he meant. Regina drew herself up stiffly. "You needn't fear I will try to thrust myself on you again. I quite understand that you want nothing to do with me."

"If your newfound humility weren't so pathetic, I'd be tempted to wring your neck. But that was my error in the first place. I forgot that Regina Cressley cannot bend gracefully. She must cover her vulnerability with pride."

"My pride has been sufficiently humbled, my lord. You rejected me most explicitly the last time we met."

"I did not reject you, only your cheap compromise. You dared not risk more, I realized later; I might have accepted it. As it was I almost took you up on that ridiculous offer."

"But you didn't," Regina said pointedly. "Moral scruples, no doubt."

"Regina, my darling idiot, my scruples, or lack of them, never entered the picture. If I hadn't wanted to strangle you at that moment, I might have taken you then and there, and damned the consequences."

"I'm not sure what consequences you think might have developed, but what possible good would it have done to rape me on the library floor?"

"Hardly rape. You were most willing."

"I lost my head, that's all."

"But you wouldn't have lost much more. We might have been able, in the throes of passion, to resolve our differences. At least then you would have been open to persuasion. But you ran off before I could marshal my offense. That was not fair of you, Regina."

"I thought I was making an ignominious retreat."

"On the contrary. You charged out of the priory with all guns blazing. I'm afraid your last salvo left me wounded on the battlefield, my armor temporarily spiked. Nevertheless I am resourceful and persistent. This proxy is my answer, my pledge in parchment that I love you exactly the way you are."

"You love me?" She managed it in barely a whisper.

"Naturally. Why else would I have gone to the trouble of coercing your rattle-pated friend John Lassiter into selling the stock to me instead of to one of your real competitors? It took a bit of gentle arm-twisting and a pointed reminder that the British attaché in Rome is my second cousin. I was forced to exert some pressure before Thwait got to him with another sort of blackmail. John didn't really want to sell to him, and he was quite happy to have that burden off his conscience."

"But why didn't you let me buy it? I was in agony not hearing a word, then discovering I had been beaten by a secret third party. And where were you these last weeks?"

"In Rome, of course, settling my accounts. As to letting you buy it, I had a better idea. Since your doubts of me all stem from the fear that once I have you in my arms, your life will cease to be your own, I decided that the only way to overcome your anxiety was to insure my guarantee in a purely professional manner. As you are conversant with contracts and warranties, you should have no trouble accepting my surety, duly signed and endorsed by a notary, that my promises are not empty air, subject to change without notice."

Regina tried not to look at him. He wasn't buying her off with a business proposition, nor attempting to topple her from her dragonlike throne. Every suspect move he had made was out of love for her and carried no more serious threat than that. But now she was back at square one. Fate had given her a second chance, and she was still too fearful to reach out and take what was hers for the asking. Her mother had told her to take the plunge, that Alistair would catch her. Yet, suppose he slipped under her weight?

"Nothing is changed," she murmured.

"Hear me out, love, before you give up on us. With that paper you hold not only my promise, but my heart. I have laid it out before you as a lovelorn swain would pay you a tribute with poetry. I am no banker holding your promissory note. You have before you my sworn pledge to guard your independence. After such an investment—and believe me, your John Lassiter drives a hard bargain—it would ill-behoove me to hamper the very person who could increase its worth. That would be a folly, and I am not rich enough to indulge in extravagance of that magnitude. But I am a wily investor and I do believe you will exercise your well-known acumen in my behalf. If I expected you to become a bustling housewife, that would be impossible. So you see my dilemma; I cannot afford to marry an ordinary woman. I need a business tycoon."

Regina looked at him lovingly, but her tone was severe. "That is the silliest argument for marriage that I have ever heard. You want me to increase your net worth."

"That should be highly appealing to you, Regina."

"Aren't you concerned that your friends in the working class will accuse you of being a grasping capitalist?"

"Ah, but my associates in the fight for women's enfranchisement will herald me as a great democrat."

Regina shook her head helplessly. "How am I to believe in such a promise? It might be counterfeit."

"Or at the very least inflationary. I understand your qualms, my love, but it wouldn't be the first time you've ventured to speculate."

"I've never gambled with my life," Regina protested. It was a frightening thought. Despite Alistair's coating the issue in imaginative terminology, no amount of contracts or promises could eliminate the human factors. "You might change your mind after a few months of being yoked to a well-oiled business machine."

"Darling girl, you are far from being a machine, though your mind works like one. Look at me, Regina. I've just applied all the logic I can muster. The next step is for me to kiss away all your misgivings. Don't try to think too much. Feeling is important too."

"Our differences won't disappear when you kiss me, Alistair."

"They don't have to. Differences are the spice of life. We'll work them out as we go along. And I won't ask you to change your ways. After all, you haven't asked me to change mine."

"But you're a man."

"And you're a woman. So? I recognize your equality. Why don't you believe me when I say it? Are only women's pledges trustworthy? It hurts me that you place so little faith in my word. Even that piece of paper doesn't still your doubts. My motives aren't so terrible. I only want to marry you."

Regina looked anything but businesslike at that moment as she rubbed her hand across her cheek. "But it won't work."

"The lady repeats herself. Of course it will work. You thought so, too, when you came to see me that disastrous afternoon. If only I hadn't lost my temper when you waved that confounded telegram under my nose! You see, I could hardly sympathize when I knew, none better, that you had nothing to fear from the sale of those shares. But I thought you wanted me to play second best, when all the time I was aiming for first fiddle. I almost didn't hear you when you said it wasn't important. But that's why I'm here now. I'm gambling on the chance that you really meant it."

"I told you I was carried away, Alistair. Of course, it was important to me."

"I'm not attempting to minimize it, just put it in perspective. You wanted me as well."

His eyes bore into hers, and Regina had to admit the truth. "It was a smokescreen of sorts. I wasn't sure of you."

"Poor Regina. Still doubting? Very well, let's clear the air. The only relationship I ever desired with you comes with a gold ring, a few orange blossoms, and a lifetime guarantee of happiness."

"How was I to know you meant marriage? Alistair Debenham and the Earl of Grantham might not have been of the same mind. You never said so."

"I said it a thousand times, but you weren't listening. Here it goes again, my love. Will you marry me?"

Regina did not answer. She wanted to with all her being, but her throat was closed tight.

"My guarantee is on that paper," he reminded her with gentle patience.

She glanced at the proxy and wondered why she wasn't already in his arms, grasping her happiness with greedy hands. When she finally answered, her voice was husky with emotion. "I'll retain my position in the business, but what about you? How can I be a wife to you at the same time? Oh, Alistair, you'll begin hating me when I say I'm needed here. Think of the resentment you'll feel when you expect a quiet weekend at home with a doting wife to cater to you, and I'm stuck in the office, hundreds of miles away, with a desk full of work. There's no solution. I can't do both."

Their eyes met across the six feet of table between them. But the real barrier that separated them could not be bridged as easily.

"Do you love me?" he asked.

"Desperately."

"Then trust me."

CHAPTER FOURTEEN

The offices of Cressley Limited were nearly empty. Almost everyone had gone home, since the reception held at eleven thirty for the staff signaled an early departure. The buff envelopes with a generous Christmas bonus enclosed had been gratefully received and their employer duly toasted with temperance eggnog. Only Regina and Miss Hodgekiss were left in the executive offices, while downstairs, Mr. Malone, the doorman, waited impatiently to lock up.

Miss Hodgekiss examined the gold watch pinned to her bosom and clicked her tongue. Rising from her desk, she knocked at the door to her employer's office.

"Come in, Dottie."

Miss Hodgekiss entered, but Regina did not look up. "Yes?" she said, her attention still on the papers in front of her.

"It's one o'clock," her secretary announced meaningfully.

"Yes, yes. Don't worry. I'll be done in a moment."

Miss Hodgekiss was stern. "Now, Miss Regina, you mustn't miss the train. There's no five o'clock special on Christmas Eve."

"But I have my cases here. I'll take a hansom straight to the station."

"I don't suppose the horses can fly either," her secretary remarked grimly.

Regina looked up at that and smiled. "Just give me five more minutes and don't fuss," she coaxed.

"Hmph." Her secretary turned away. "You'll work yourself to death one of these days, that's what," she predicted gloomily as she shut the door with what came perilously close to a bang.

Regina bent her head over the papers once more, and for some time the only sound in the room was the busy scratch of her pen. Her white blouse was mostly hidden by a dark green vest, while her gray wool skirt was bare of any ornamentation. The lustrous brown hair was caught up in its usual severe topknot, but a few rebellious wisps had escaped to lie softly on the nape of her white neck. Finally Regina stacked her papers with brisk competence and thrust them into a folder. About to put that into a capacious and rather worn briefcase beside her, she hesitated, then left it on the desk. It was Christmas after all. There was enough in the case as it was. She stood up, stretched, and surveyed her inky fingers ruefully before seeing the time. The fat little clock on her desk pointed with seeming smugness to one fifteen.

"Oh, no!" she wailed. The briefcase forgotten, Regina grabbed her coat from the closet and jammed her stylish fur hat on her head with uncharacteristic carelessness. Tearing through the outer office, she paused only to hug the faithful Dottie and call a breathless "Happy Christmas" over her shoulder.

"Mr. Malone, quick!" she panted. But Miss Hodgekiss had been as efficient as ever. A cab was waiting at the curb with her cases already loaded in the back and the doorman waiting to hand her up the steps.

"Thank you," she gasped as Dottie gave her the forgotten briefcase, and the cab took off with a jerk.

"One of these days she'll cut it too fine," Miss Hodgekiss said dourly to Malone as the cab whirled around the corner, the horses already at a run.

"A real character she is," Malone remarked with satisfaction.

Miss Hodgekiss disapproved of the familiarity. "You mean, she has character," she snapped. "Though what all this dashing about will do to her I'd not like to think. She's not here half the time and when she is, she works like a demon. I never thought I'd be the one to tell her to stop speaking for the Cause, but she's taken on too much lately."

"Whatever she does, it certainly seems to agree with her. The lady smiles all the time now. But ain't you ready to leave, miss?" the doorman hinted broadly, anxious to get home and imbibe a little Christmas cheer. Temperance eggnog was not his idea of a drink.

"Certainly, Malone. I'll just get my coat." Miss

Hodgekiss hurried upstairs. She had a train to catch herself, as she was spending Christmas with Miss Wingarten, as usual. Gazing around the familiar office before switching off the light, she smiled unconsciously. A few months earlier she had come close to losing her place in it and it was doubly dear in consequence.

Chuff offered the Earl of Grantham his coat just as Big Ben struck three o'clock. "A very merry Christmas, m'lord," he said as he helped his master slide one arm into a flannel-lined sleeve.

Alistair turned around to take his hat and umbrella. "Happy Christmas, Chuff."

"It certainly will be, thanks to you, sir." Chuff patted the pocket where the earl's gift reposed.

"I'm looking forward to what I believe is my best Christmas ever," Lord Grantham said cheerfully. "A pretty wife makes a great deal of difference, doesn't she, Chuff? But then you've been telling me that for years."

"Pretty is as pretty does, m'lord," Chuff said heartily, thinking of his own fat and homely, well-loved Bess at home.

"I'll tell my countess that she can no longer rely on her looks to turn me sweet, shall I?"

"Never say that I told you," Chuff protested in horror.

The earl laughed and departed, leaving his office manager to close up. Chuff hoped the Earl would not pass his remark on to the countess, as that lady was indeed the epitome of all that was desirable in a wife. Though Lord Grantham still spent far too much time in the city, it was a great relief to Chuff that the gentleman had such a sweet thing to go home to each weekend. The countess was ever so solicitous of her husband's well-being and the first to remind him that the empire would not collapse if he left early on a Friday afternoon. Yes, sir, she was a right'un, not that the earl didn't deserve the very best, for there wasn't a man to match him anywhere, or likely to be.

Perhaps it would snow, the vicar thought happily as he looked up at the gray skies and loosened the woolly muffler around his neck, heedless as a child at the danger and inconvenience of a winter storm. Wiping his feet, he entered the side door of the priory and sniffed appreciatively. Gingerbread. Miss Margaret would no doubt send some in with his tea. Heading down the hall toward the library, he passed the open door of the drawing room. The sound of laughter made him peer in at a charming sight. Celia was handing one end of a red ribbon to Tom, who was perched high on a stepladder.

"Mistletoe!" the vicar said approvingly just as Tom claimed a kiss from his young wife.

Celia turned around with a blush of pleasure. "Papa!" she exclaimed. "Has Miss Margaret put you to work too?"

"Oh, no. I just came to consult one of Lord Grantham's books for my sermon tomorrow."

"Better not let Miss Margaret see you," Tom warned, "or you'll be set to work decorating the tree or lugging in flowers from the conservatory."

"I suppose I could lend a hand," the vicar said doubtfully. "It's so kind of the earl to invite me here for Christmas."

"Yes, isn't it grand?" Celia agreed, her eyes on Tom's progress with the ribbon. "Dear, that bow is hanging just a little crooked. That's better."

Arthur Cressley stood hesitant for a moment, then slipped an arm around his daughter and stole a shy kiss under the mistletoe for himself.

"Dear Papa." Celia patted him affectionately on the arm. "Are you all right? Are you lonely over at the vicarage with me gone?"

"How could I be when you come over every day to check up on Mrs. Gatchell, and I have dinner at the Grange with you often as not?" he asked wonderingly as he headed for the doorway.

But before he was out of the room, Miss Margaret had entered. "Oh, there you are, Mr. Cressley," she said, smiling. "I've sent Gladys to the library with some gingerbread for you. But come and give me your opinion. James has brought in the tree. Tell me if you think it is in the right place. You too, Celia, Tom."

The tree, tall and thick with spicy-scented needles, stood naked in the hall, while the staircase and gallery above it were already hung with holly laced with scarlet ribbons.

"We've always put it in the corner by the stairs,

but perhaps this time we should pull it out toward the center."

"It's very pretty," the vicar said noncommittally. Privately he felt that the yule log and the hanging of the greens were the more authentic English customs, and deplored the tree as a German intrusion.

Celia was quite decided. "It's perfect just where it is, Miss Margaret. Lord and Lady Grantham will be delighted."

Tom groaned. "It's absolutely enormous. How are we to have it ready by six o'clock? Isn't that when they arrive?"

"Yes, I expect them on the six-ten from London. But don't worry. James will help you," Miss Margaret said cheerfully. "Ah, here you are, James. Put those boxes over there. The ornaments. I packed them away myself last year."

The vicar faded back to his books before he could be recruited to help with the decorations. There were enough hands without him, and after all, the sermon was the most important part of the Christmas service. It was necessary to polish it to perfection.

Miss Margaret lingered, giving excellent instructions. The Christmas festivities were planned to the last detail, and she had no doubt that all would go as smoothly as usual. Years as her brother's political hostess made this family party a mere sinecure, though the logistics were complicated enough. The house had been shut up for more than a month before she arrived last Saturday to organize things. Now all was polished and prepared, the larder filled, the menus planned down to the wines served with each course, and the choices made for which flowers to go on the breakfast trays.

"Will Lady Grantham be pleased?" Celia asked as she helped wind a streamer artistically through the green branches. "What a shame she couldn't be here to help with the preparations."

"The dear girl never criticizes my plans," Miss Margaret smiled complacently, "and she always compliments me on the way things look, but I'm not at all sure she notices much unless it's directly under her nose. The last time they were here, I was trying out a new French chef. He was a genius, except when he was into the wine. The first evening everything was either burnt or sauced with garlic, and I didn't know how to apologize. Of course, she told me it was all delicious. It's Alistair who keeps me up to the mark."

"Perhaps she doesn't complain because everything is just about perfect."

"Well, I do try," Margaret preened, confident in the knowledge that her place was unassailed. Alistair's wife wisely refrained from interfering in the one area of his life that only his sister could fill. That attitude went a long way in keeping up their friendly relationship. "Of course," Margaret continued, "she knows she's a lucky girl to have me to take care of things for her. She has no more idea of what it takes to run a household this size than a child. Celia, I'd wait until I finished the streamers before hanging those glass balls, if I were you. Now I must see that the punch bowl is filled for the carolers." Miss Margaret hurried off.

Celia and Tom worked on until the Debenhams' imposing butler brought them hot spiced cider and some of the gingerbread that had delighted the vicar. Sitting down on the sofa by the hall fireplace, where a cheerful coal fire flickered in the darkening afternoon, they munched hungrily.

"What a wonderful Christmas this is going to be," Celia said drowsily, mesmerized by the dancing flames.

"Because we're together," Tom agreed, drawing her close. "Funny, wasn't it, their getting married. I had no idea he was even attracted to her."

Celia was amused. She knew who he meant, of course. "Don't you think she is attractive?" she asked.

"Not my type," he responded, kissing the tip of her nose.

"We were too busy with our problems to notice, weren't we? Still, I saw it, though I never dreamed he would actually propose. Old as Lord Grantham is, I assumed he was a confirmed bachelor."

"It's nice to think that when we're old like him, we'll still care. Well, look at my parents. They seem so happy together now."

"They're sweet," Celia agreed. But then Tom insisted on getting up and finishing the tree so they would have time to rest and dress before coming back for dinner there that night.

"Slave driver," she complained.

Barclay had been right, Tom thought fleetingly. Celia had thoroughly domesticated him. He no longer went up to London but was quite content to stay in Grantly, helping his father with the estate, spending quiet evenings with his wife. In fact, it suited him, he realized. Tom had gotten over his anger at Tristam, and although Barclay's permanent departure from Honeysuckle Cottage was a relief to the Dawlishes, Tom seldom thought of his former friend. Barclay was in the south of France these days they heard, but with scant interest.

The snow began to fall heavily sometime that afternoon and, in consequence, the six-ten was late. James had taken the carriage to the station but returned without the earl and his wife. It seemed there would be a delay of an hour and a half at least.

Philosophically Miss Margaret put dinner back and continued her last-minute inspection of the house. Lord and Lady Grantham's suite was in perfect order and charmingly decorated with holly on the mantelpiece and poinsettia in the lady's boudoir, redecorated for her with mauve silk hangings and a white bearskin rug. It still embarrassed Margaret slightly that her brother and his wife had adopted the unfashionable custom of sharing the same bedroom. His robe hanging on the bedstead added a certain intimacy that made

Margaret feel as if she were intruding. Yet she couldn't deny a certain satisfaction from it. Margaret was surprisingly fond of her brother's bride. They got along well, perhaps because both of them were determined that Alistair should be happy. That shared goal, well established by now, Margaret thought, was reason enough to bring them together. What was a potentially explosive situation had slipped naturally into a division of interests. Her sister-in-law was content to leave all the domestic arrangements in Margaret's capable hands while she devoted herself to other aspects of marriage. Both parties were very satisfied with this state of affairs, and Margaret soon fell into the habit of taking credit for sponsoring what was, after all, a love match.

Closing the door carefully behind her, she descended to the main floor, where all was in readiness. The dining room table was set with the finest Wedgwood and crystal, a silver epergne filled with Christmas roses on the sideboard. In the hall the Christmas tree stood in all its traditional splendor, brightly wrapped packages piled at its feet, while several smaller ones hung invitingly from the sturdier branches. The candles, clipped here and there, were as yet unlit. The second footman was to kindle them only on Margaret's signal soon after the dessert plates were cleared away. Margaret looked complacently at the gifts. She had purchased something small but elegant for each of the guests invited tonight, and Alistair was sure to approve her choices.

Shortly after six thirty the guests began to arrive and Margaret was engrossed in the bustle of greeting them. The vicar came not long after the Dawlishes, and soon everyone, glass in hand, was settled in the elegant drawing room. The squire had managed to kiss all the ladies under the mistletoe, even luring his wife back under the golden leaves for another hearty buss on the lips.

"And where are the earl and his blushing bride?" he demanded jovially.

"The snow has caused certain delays in the train schedule, but James is waiting at the station to bring them home," Margaret explained.

"Regina is coming, isn't she?" the vicar asked a little vaguely.

"Yes, Papa, of course she is," Celia answered with infinite patience.

Lady Telford spoke up. "Tomorrow she's going to address the Mother's Union on the question of votes for women. As it is Boxing Day, I expect a grand turnout."

"Of women," Tom laughed. "I'd not step near the place."

"But you promised," Celia reminded him.

Catherine Eliot resolved the matter. "We will need you if anyone becomes rowdy, Mr. Dawlish. You would not want your young wife subjected to unseemly behavior."

"No, of course not." Tom was rather flattered that he should be asked to play Sir Galahad for a group of defenseless women, and Mrs. Eliot smiled to herself.

"Besides," Celia admonished, "Regina is your cousin, too, now, and she deserves your support."

"Lord Grantham will be there, no doubt," the squire said. "Emancipation is one of his pet causes. I think I will come also," he decided handsomely. "Always wanted to hear one of those suffragettes."

Miss Margaret protested his terminology. "Suffragette! I deplore the name. It's so vulgar."

"That's what the newspapers are beginning to call us, Margaret. You might as well get used to it," Lady Telford stated. "By the way, I've succeeded in recruiting Mrs. Thwait. She's agreed to contribute a good sum toward the cost of circulating our petition, so you must relent now and invite her to your next affair."

Margaret glared at her best friend. "I knew as soon as you took hold of Regina's idea of a petition that this sort of thing would develop. The Thwaits have been a byword since their son ran off with that unprincipled hussy. Now you expect me to receive the woman."

"The Cause requires such sacrifices," Mrs. Eliot chided. "And you can't blame the parents if two youngsters decide they are in love. It happens every day. Look at your brother."

Mrs. Dawlish reached impulsively for her wine glass, toppling it over in her haste. "Yes, anyone could see they were in love."

No one was sure if she meant the runaway Thwaits or the Earl of Grantham and his wife, but in either case she was correct, and Celia mopped up the small stain unobtrusively.

Margaret ignored the accident, as she was still intent on her own grievance. "After all I did for that child. And then she behaved like a wanton. Poor Bella nearly went into a decline over the affair, as well she should. It was in this very room that she found Dimity's note."

The vicar was puzzled. "A wanton? What did Miss Farnsworth do? She seemed a sweet child."

Celia explained quickly. "Don't you remember, Papa? She ran away with Stephen Thwait, and they were married by special license."

"A hole-in-corner affair," Margaret sniffed.

"Yes, but that wasn't wanton," the vicar considered seriously. "Ill-advised perhaps, and disrespectful of her family, but hardly immoral. You did say they are married, so how can—"

"Never mind, Papa," Celia interrupted. "It's all settled now."

"Young people will please themselves," Catherine Eliot said in a pertinent reminder to Miss Margaret that the best laid plans can go astray. "And if the Farnsworths aren't happy to accept the Thwaits as family, their money is respectable enough. Darling Dimity will be able to cut quite a swathe through society in diamonds."

No more was said on the topic, for just then the drawing room doors were thrown open, and the impassive butler announced the arrival of the Earl and Countess of Grantham at last.

They stood at the threshold, a slight powdering

of snow still clinging to their outer clothes. Jenkins divested the countess of her white ermine cape and fur hat before helping the earl off with his things. It was then that everyone noticed the emerald collar adorning Lady Grantham's elegant throat. Alistair's Christmas gift, no doubt, and a perfect foil for his wife's dark beauty. Indeed, the Countess of Grantham carried her position with regal elegance, though her eyes were warm with a special kind of contentment. She was radiant in green silk and finely pleated lace, but no more so than her husband, distinguished, as always, in formal black dinner clothes. Their eyes met warmly before they greeted their guests. How grand they were. So handsome and so in love.

There were hugs and kisses and a rush of happy chatter, each anxious to bring the others up-to-date on whatever happenings had ensued since they had last met.

"A telegram came today from Aunt Virginia and her new husband," Celia said. "A terrible snow storm in Paris has held up all the trains, and they won't be able to get away for a few days at least. I'm so disappointed," she lamented. "And, of course, you know Great-Aunt Pen is speaking in Edinburgh the day after tomorrow, so she won't be here until afterwards. But isn't it wonderful that the rest of us are all together?" She beamed.

The countess gave her a warm hug. "You're simply glowing, my dear, and I daresay, it isn't the snow outside that's given you an extra bloom on your cheeks."

Celia savored the knowledge to herself. It would be soon enough to make her announcement once the excitement of the Granthams' return had died down. New Year's Day would be an appropriate time to disclose that the Dawlishes were expecting an addition to the family.

Alistair gave his sister an affectionate kiss on the cheek. "The house looks lovely, Margaret. You've surpassed yourself. But where is dinner? I'm starving."

"A fine thing it isn't burnt to a crisp by now," she chided. "The both of you certainly took your time about getting here."

"I realize you think I'm omnipotent, sister, but snow is somewhat outside my jurisdiction. There are things more powerful than the Earl of Grantham, you know."

"Yes," laughed Lady Telford. "The Countess of Grantham. You've never looked better, Alistair. Marriage agrees with you."

"My wife agrees with me. And I'm sure she'll also agree that it is time we all sat down to one of Margaret's inimitable feasts."

"I'm very glad you both had the sense to change clothes at the London house before coming here, or we'd have another hour's wait before dinner," his sister grumbled.

"My wife is an organizational genius," he teased. "Almost on your level." What the earl did not add was that the interlude before they finally got around to getting dressed had delayed them as much as the capricious storm outside.

Moments later the Earl of Grantham was taking his seat at the head of the table. He caught his wife's eye and raised his wine glass to her in a silent salute. She smiled back, her heart accelerating to an alarming degree at the look her husband was giving her. After six months of marriage her response to him was as immoderate as ever. She turned her hot cheeks away from the suggestion in his eyes and concentrated instead on what the squire was saying.

He was already standing and raising his glass for a toast. "To our charming host and hostess," he boomed. "A most perfect union, arranged by the gods . . . and Miss Debenham," he winked broadly. "To them . . . the lord and lady of the manor . . . as gracious as they are loving. To Alistair and Regina."

There was general acclamation for his sentiments, and immediately the first course was carried in. They began with oysters.

INTRODUCING...

The Romance Magazine For The 1980's

Each exciting issue contains a full-length romance novel — the kind of first-love story we all dream about...

___PLUS

other wonderful features such as a travelogue to the world's most romantic spots, advice about your romantic problems, a quiz to find the ideal mate for you and much, much more.

ROMANTIQUE: A complete novel of romance, plus a whole world of romantic features.

ROMANTIQUE: Wherever magazines are sold. Or write Romantique Magazine, Dept. C-1, 41 East 42nd Street, New York, N.Y. 10017

Once you've tasted joy and passion, do you dare dream of

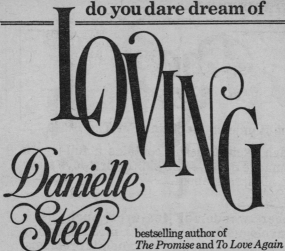

LOVING

Danielle Steel

bestselling author of
The Promise and *To Love Again*

Bettina Daniels lived in a gilded world—pampered, adored, adoring. She had youth, beauty and a glamorous life that circled the globe—everything her father's love, fame and money could buy. Suddenly, Justin Daniels was gone. Bettina stood alone before a mountain of debts and a world of strangers—men who promised her many things, who tempted her with words of love. But Bettina had to live her own life, seize her own dreams and take her own chances. But could she pay the bittersweet price?

A Dell Book ================= **$2.75 (14684-4)**

The first novel in the spectacular new
Heiress series

The English Heiress

Roberta Gellis

Leonie De Conyers—beautiful, aristocratic, she lived in the
shadow of the guillotine, stripped of everything she held
dear. Roger St. Eyre—an English nobleman, he set out to save
Leonie in a world gone mad.

They would be kidnapped, denounced and brutally separated. Driven by passion, they would escape France, return
to England, fulfill their glorious destiny and seize a lofty
dream.

A Dell Book $2.50 (12141-8)